I0535593

Secrets Of Snow Hollow

By

Lizzy Stevens

ALL RIGHTS RESERVED
No part of this book may be reproduced
or transmitted in any form or by any
means, electronic or mechanical,
including photocopying, recording, or by
any information storage and retrieval
system, without permission in writing
from the author, except in the case of
brief quotations embodied in reviews.

Publishers Note:
This is a work of fiction. All names,
characters, places, and events are the
work of the author's imagination.
Any resemblance to real persons, places,
or events is coincidental.

Solstice Publishing ©2010

Table Of Contents

Book One
Jenna's Story

Chapter One

Jenna Addison looked up at the moon and felt uneasy. She was only six years old, but she knew things that other people didn't. She had not yet come into her full powers. She couldn't pinpoint exactly what would happen, but she knew how to read the signs —the leaves on the trees all turned upside down, and the red glowing ring around the moon.

There were other things too. Most people would walk right past not even realizing any of it, but Jenna was different. Her entire family was different. Her sister Jamie was four and Jackie was two. Their parents wanted children close in age so they would feel close to each other as they grew. When her parents told her that, Jenna did not quite understand, but she knew she loved her sisters very much.

Today was Jenna's sixth birthday, and she was expecting her grandmother to show up. She had to talk to her about the signs. Her grandmother would know what to do. She always knew what to do.

When Grandma pulled into the drive, Jenna took off running. "Grandma Elena. I'm so glad you're here. I've been waiting for you."

Elena Hastings—a strong woman who never seemed to age—didn't look a day older than forty. But in fact she was sixty. "Hello, Dear. How is my big grown up granddaughter today on her birthday?" She scooped her up into a big bear hug.

Jenna loved her grandmother dearly. "Grandma, I need to talk to you. I saw some signs today."

"I know honey. I've seen them too. It's not good. You should prepare yourself for bad news." She pulled her granddaughter in closer.

"But Grandma, what is going to happen?" She knew that her grandmother knew more than she was telling.

"I don't know sweetie, but it's something bad. I can't get a reading on it, which tells me that it's about me or somebody close to me."

Jenna could see the concern in her grandmother's eyes. All the signs told her something bad would happen that evening, but they didn't tell her what the bad thing would be. Jenna went to bed that night knowing things would be different in the morning.

She heard her grandmother crying. It woke her in the middle of the night, and she ran downstairs, yelling, "Grandma, what is it? What's wrong?"

Jenna stood there starring at her grandma. She saw her tears coming and felt her own building up inside. Something bad had happened to her parents. She could feel it. The look on her grandma's face told her everything she needed to know. Silence filled the air, and Jenna wanted to go back in time somehow. She didn't know what happened, but she knew it wasn't good.

She stood there still as she could be as she listened to her grandmother explain to her that her parents were dead. It was a car crash. A drunk driver had ran a stop light and hit them head on. The police report said they died instantly. Jenna's whole body started to shake as she stood in her living room listening to her whole world crumble in front of her. Everything was about to change. *People always say change if for the good, but did those people every loose both of their parents, she wondered.*

"You girls are going to be just fine. I will take care of you."

Jenna wiped the tears away from her face. "What do you mean, Grandma? What's going to happen to us?"

Elena looked down at the precious

child. "You will go back to Snow Hollow with me of course."

* * *

Jenna wiped her tears as she awoke in a strange bed, sobbing and calling for Mommy. But Mommy didn't answer. She called to Daddy. But no one came. The hurting in her chest was back again, and her breath came in short gasps as she sat up and looked around the room. Minutes passed before she remembered.

Then she reminded herself her parents could never come back. Never again. Grandma had said so—and Grandma always knew.

But Jenna also knew that her grandmother loved her very much and would take good care of her. And when she walked into Jamie and Jackie's room and saw them there in peaceful sleep, she was sure Grandma would take great care of them too. And a little bit of her pain went away.

The smell of bacon filled the air as Jenna walked down the stairs. Grandma stood at the kitchen stove.

"Hello my dear child. How are you feeling this morning?"

Jenna smiled up at her. "I'm okay Grandma."

"Jenna, Honey. I know things are different right now and you're sad, but I promise you in time things will be better. It may not seem like it now, but they will."

Jenna fought back tears as she sat at the table and ate in silence. She loved her grandmother but-didn't feel like talking.

When Elena went to check on her sisters, Jenna sat alone in the kitchen and looked around with a sense that someone else was there. The strange, new sensation made her feel comfortable and safe, and not afraid.

Elena came back to the kitchen minutes later as Jenna placed her dish in the sink.

"Jenna Honey. I want to talk to you for a minute. Do you ever have feelings like the one you had on your birthday?

"Sometimes. I feel things." Jenna said as she glanced around the kitchen again. Still not sure what she felt in that room.

"What kind of things?" Elena asked.

Jenna shrugged her shoulders. "I don't know. It's hard to tell you what I mean. Like right now. I feel like somebody is in the room with us, but I can't see anyone."

Elena looked over at her granddaughter and smiled deep inside. She was right about her. She hadn't seen it in the other two girls, but she saw it in Jenna. The other two may be too young or they may never have the gift that Jenna does. Only time would tell.

"Okay, sweetie. I was just wondering. You can go play now. I'll clean up the kitchen."

Jenna and her sisters ran and laughed and played in the fenced back yard where the little ones could not wander off. The most beautiful bluebird Jenna had ever seen rested on the birdbath. Jenna held out her hand as she walked toward it, and the bird landed on her hand. Jenna looked up and smiled. "I won't hurt you."

Seconds later, the bird flew away. But as Elena watched from the porch, she knew Jenna had a way with nature. It was going to be easier than she thought to train her. This child had a very special gift, and it would be Elena's job to teach Jenna how to use her gift.

Jamie and Jackie sat in the sand box building sand castles, but Jenna fed the squirrels and birds. It was as if she was talking to them and they understood her. As Elena stood and watched she couldn't be sure how much power Jenna had but she knew she would grow up to be much more powerful than herself.

* * *

Elena put the younger girls to bed for an afternoon nap, then went to Jenna's room, where she sat on the floor playing with her Barbie doll.

She looked up. "Hi Grandma. Want to play?"

Elena smiled . "Sure Jenna. I would love to play. I want to teach you a secret way that you can only play with me."

Jenna was very excited by all the secrecy. "Okay Grandma. How do you play?"

Elena had to know if Jenna had any powers yet. "Jenna, see that car for your doll over by the door?" I want you to hold out your hand and then tell that car to come to your hand."

Jenna did as she said, but the car did not move.

"Okay Jenna. Now I want you to think real hard that you want that car to come to your hand."

Jenna stared at the car and thought as hard as she could. The car started moving toward her.

"Grandma, how is this happening?"

Elena smiled with joy. She was right. Jenna was very gifted. Her powers were starting at an early age. Jenna would not get her full powers until she was twenty- six. Elena wouldn't tell her everything until then. No need for her to worry about what lies ahead.

Back in the kitchen, Elena planned protection potions to scatter around the house. She would have to protect those girls with everything she had. Once the underworld found out they were there their lives would be in danger. But she would not bother them with that sooner than necessary. Their lives should be as normal as possible.

Elena filled her tea kettle. She loved the smell of apple cinnamon tea brewing on the stove top.

"I have to protect the girls."

Jenna came running in the door for a cold drink. "Who are you talking to Grandma?"

Elena looked up from her tea kettle. "Nobody. I was just talking to myself."

Jenna laughed. "You're silly Grandma. I'm going back out to play."

As Jenna ran out, Elena spoke to the spirit of a man who appeared in the room. "They have so much energy now. Don't they?"

"They sure do. It is now your job to protect them with all that you have. You are not alone in this battle. Remember this."

"I know." Elena said. "I only wish that they didn't have to have this battle. At least they have time to prepare for it. I'm working on a potion now to protect them."

Elena knew that she had to get back into her regular life routine. She had a very successful magic shop. Most people in the town thought it was a fun place to buy candles and scents and things. Elena made decent money and it gave her a reason to order supplies for spells and things without drawing attention to herself. She could simply say that it was for the shop. Nobody ever questioned it.

She would be interviewing nannies in a day or two to take care of Jaimie and Jackie. Jenna would go to the shop with Elena where she could be taught more about her gift. She needed to know how to protect herself.

Elena went to the back door. "Girls. It's time to come in and get cleaned up for dinner."

The girls came running. They never argued about it, which was a nice surprise.

"Grandma, do you need any help with dinner?" Jenna asked.

"Of course my dear. You can always

help me."

Elena put Jackie in the high chair and then the rest of them sat down to a nice dinner. She loved to cook.

Chapter two

9 Years Later

Elena's intuition told her it was time to begin Jenna's training. She was fifteen and old enough to understand that the impossible could become possible.

Elena dropped Jamie and Jackie off at dance class and her and Jenna drove home. Jenna never showed any interest in dance. Elena knew it was because she had a much bigger purpose in life.

They pulled into the drive. Elena turned to Jenna and said. "Jenna. I think it's time for us to have a long talk."

"Did I do something wrong Grandma?"

"Oh, no Honey. You could never do anything wrong. I simply want to talk to you about something important."

Elena put on some tea and got Jenna and herself both a cup. This was going to be a long talk. She was about to explain to her granddaughter that the reason she knew certain things was because she was a witch. She knew her granddaughter was going to look at her oddly. She had never labeled Jenna's gift as being a witch. She grabbed them both some cookies from the cupboard to help ease into the conversation.

Jenna looked up at Elena with a serious look on her face. She could tell that something was wrong. "What is it, Grandma?"

Elena let out a sigh. "Jenna, Honey. You

know how you know things and you can think really hard about something and things might move slightly?"

"Yeah, why?"

"Well Honey. The thing is... This is very difficult for me to explain. So I'm just going to blurt it out and then we will go from there. You are a witch. I am a witch and your mother was a witch. There I've said it."

Jenna looked at her grandmother like she had lost her mind. "Uh, Grandma, are you okay? You are talking crazy. I'm not a witch. I can't do any spells or anything."

"Jenna. You are only fifteen. I have only begun to show you little things because it will be many years before you can fully use your gift. I will teach you as much as you want to learn. I do promise you that, but there is a catch. You can't tell anyone. This has to be kept a secret. No one must know. Do you understand?"

"Yes, Grandma. I can't think of any reason why I would want to tell people that I'm a witch. I don't need burned at the stake." She chuckled.

The two sat there for at least an hour talking before they left to go pick up the girls from dance practice.

Elena knew that with the other two girls going to dance practice three days a week, that would allow her and Jenna some time alone for her to teach Jenna how to use her gift.

She spent the next few days in the attic deciding what spells would be the easiest for Jenna to work on. Her skills may not work for another year or more, but Elena had to start somewhere.

She found a few very simple things to start with such as turning a wilted rose back into a healthy rose. She thought that would be perfect. They would start first thing in the morning.

"Girls. It's time for bed."

The moans and groan from the other room started. They were at the ages that they hated bedtime. It was a choir to get them in bed.

"Oh, can't we finish this movie?" Jamie asked in a whining voice.

"What movie is it?" Elena wanted to know what was so interesting that they couldn't got to bed on time.

Jamie took a minute before answering.

"I don't know the name. I just started watching it and I missed the first half, but it looks really good."

"Okay girls. I think you should probably go ahead and go to bed. We will have to find out what the name of the movie is and rent it if it's that good."

The girls reluctantly went to bed. They knew it was an argument they wouldn't win anyway.

As Jenna lay in bed that night, she had a hard time falling asleep. Her whole life was about to change. She had always known that she was different, but she would never have guessed how different. Jenna rolled onto her stomach trying to get comfortable. Closing her eyes, she felt a tingle go up her spine. She had felt it many times throughout her life but never the way it felt tonight. Tonight it was almost tangible, like someone was standing right above her with their hand on her back in a comforting gesture. Jenna quickly rolled over to her back, but no one was there.

The next morning Elena got up and fixed the girls a big breakfast. It was Sunday and her shop was closed. She planned to work on spells with Jenna that morning. Jamie and Jackie would be busy practicing for their dance recital.

Jenna came walking down the stairs bright and early. "Good Morning, Grandma. Can I help with breakfast?"

Elena was putting the last of the food onto the table. "I'm all done. I just need to make myself some apple cinnamon tea. I can't have my breakfast without my tea." She smiled.

Jenna loved the smell of her tea cooking. The aroma filled the house and made her feel safe in some crazy way. She never really understood why.

When they finished breakfast Elena told Jamie and Jackie to go practice and her and Jenna headed to the attic.

"What are we doing Grandma?"

Elena looked over at her granddaughter. "I want to show you something. Remember what I've said before though. Never tell a soul about the things I show you."

Jenna had no idea what was going on but she nodded in agreement.

"Okay, Honey. See this wilted dying rose?"

Jenna looked at the saddest thing she had ever seen. It was a wilted red rose. It didn't look happy or loved anymore. It almost brought a tear to her eye. "Yes, I see it. What about it?"

"Jenna. I want you to look at it very hard. With all of your heart and mind, I want you to tell this flower that you love it and it needs to come back to you now."

Jenna thought her grandma was crazy. Did she honestly believe that she was going to be able to bring this flower back to life. Jenna didn't want to disappoint her grandma so she looked at the rose.

Jenna stared at it and truly with all of her heart she said. "You are the most beautiful rose that I have ever seen. You are loved and it's not your time to die. Come back to me."

Before Jenna's very eyes the rose started lifting . It was actually coming back to life. After just seconds, it was sitting straight up full of life.

"Wow! Did I do that?" Jenna was overjoyed with emotions at that very moment.

"Yes, my dear. You did." Elena said with a smile. She knew that Jenna was a very special girl.

Chapter 3

Jenna was growing into a beautiful young woman over the years and was very excited about her first real date. She had boyfriends before, but this was the first time that she was actually going out with a boy. She was going to the movies with Todd Meads. He was only the cutest boy in her entire school. At least that's what all the other girls thought.

Jenna spent hours getting ready. She stood in front of her mirror changing outfit after outfit.

Jamie sat on the bed watching her sister going crazy over the date. "Jenna. You look great. Don't worry."

Jenna looked over at her sister. "Thanks, Jamie. I just want everything to be perfect."

When it finally was , at least in her own mind, she went downstairs to wait. She waited for what seemed like hours when in all actuality it was only minutes. Then finally the door bell rang.

She was more nervous than she had ever been. They were only going to a movie and then to grab an ice cream with friends before coming back home. It wasn't a big deal and she had to be home by nine o'clock, but she was still nervous.

"Hi Todd. Come on in and meet my grandmother before we go."

"Okay Jenna, but we need to get going

soon if we are going to make the movie on time." Todd said as he glanced at his watch.

"Grandma. Would you like to meet Todd before we go."

This was bitter sweet for Elena. Her little girl was growing up. She walked in to meet the boy. "Hello. It's very nice to meet you. You two be careful tonight and be home on time."

"Yes, maam. We won't be late. I promise."

The two of them went out to Todd's car and headed to the movies as far as Jenna knew.

They drove for a little while and then Todd turned down the road leading out of town.

Jenna glanced out the window with a

feeling of uneasiness. "Todd. Where are we going? I thought we were going to a movie."

"I thought we would get to know each other a little better. There weren't any good movies playing anyway." He smiled over at her.

Jenna didn't like this at all. It made her very uncomfortable to lie to her grandmother and she didn't like not knowing where they were going.

Todd turned down an old dirt road that led down by the river. He brought the car to a stop and turned off the engine.

"Isn't it beautiful out tonight, Jenna?"

Jenna looked out the car window and had to agree, but it didn't mean she wasn't still nervous.

Todd leaned over to turn the radio on

a slow music playing station. He was setting the mood. Then he scooted closer to Jenna.

"Todd, maybe we should....."

Before she could finish, Todd leaned in and kissed her gently on the lips. He kissed her a couple of more times and then he moved to her neck.

"Todd, stop. We can't do this. I'm not ready for this step. It's our first date. I think we should go back into town."

Todd stopped and looked up at her. "Jenna. Are you going to stay a baby forever. I mean come on. All the other kids are doing it. What's the problem? We aren't little kids anymore. " He leaned in to kiss her again.

"Todd. I said, I'm not doing this. Take me home."

"I didn't know that you were such a

child. I never would have asked you out. The whole school is going to hear about this tomorrow. You're reputation will be ruined. No guy will ever ask you out again."

Jenna felt the air around her begin to chill. A tingle crawled up her spine and she turned to Todd. Todd's face was ashen.

"Todd? Todd, are you okay?"

Todd slowly turned his head toward her.

"I'm fine Jenna. I must apologize for the things I did and said to you."

"Okay...Are you sure you're okay?"

Jenna was frightened by the absence of emotion on Todd's face. He spoke as if he was a robot.

"I'm fine. But I'm a jerk and I intend to tell that to the whole school on Monday. I'm also going to tell them that you are too good for the likes of me."

Todd started the car and the air began to warm but not before Jenna felt a slight tingle on her scalp and sensation that almost felt like a caress on her hair.

Todd was quiet on the ride home but thankfully not catatonic like he was previously. Arriving back home, he quickly got out and ran around the car to open the door for Jenna. He walked her to the front door and said, "Thank you Jenna for a great evening."

With that, he turned and walked back to his car, got in and drove away.

Jenna stared after him trying to make sense when her Grandma came out and joined her.

"Was that the same guy who picked you up earlier?"

"I think so Grandma. It was weird. He tried to kiss me and all of a sudden he got a blank look on his face and said he was sorry and brought me home. I'm not sure what happened."

Jenna shrugged and went inside.

Elena stood there for a minute and then smiled and shook her head.

"Boys will be boys." She muttered before she too went inside.

Chapter Four

Jenna couldn't believe twenty years had passed since the death of her parents. Now, Jenna was burying her grandmother. She stood and stared at the mound of flowers on the ground as the rain beat down on her black umbrella. But it was not the rain that caused the chill in her spine, the knot of dread in her chest and the unbearable ache in her heart.

She and Grandma had been very close, and for most of Jenna's life, she worked in her grandmother's magic shop side by side with her. The people of Snow Hollow loved the scented candles, herbs, potions and bubble baths. No one questioned whether the family really knew magic or spells. But Jenna knew, and she carried the burden deep inside, never finding true love because she had never found anyone she could trust with the family secret.

Though she had been told her powers were a gift, they often seemed like a curse. She had foreseen the death of her own sweet grandmother, that dear old woman who had cared for her, guided her and loved her.

The same foretelling had been there—the same signs she saw the night her parents died in that awful crash—the moon encircled by a red ring, just as before.

Jenna stood in the living room of her grandmother's house not really knowing what to do next. Her sisters moved away as soon as they were old enough. They longed for bigger cities and more excitement. Jenna always felt that she was pulled to Snow Hollow for some reason. She could never quite explain it, but she knew that she belonged there.

After her sisters left, Jenna looked around the big empty two story house. She never felt more alone than she did in that very moment. Her grandmother was her best friend. Jenna knew that she needed to go through her grandmother's belongings and get rid of things that she wouldn't need, but the thought of doing it felt like a knife in her heart. She walked aimlessly around the house not knowing where to begin. Her grandmother had left her sister's some money, but Jenna had received the house, the magic shop and the biggest bulk of the money. Her grandmother always liked her best. Jenna always felt a connection to her grandmother. It couldn't be explained.

Jenna was drawn to the attic more now than ever before. She spent many hours in there with her grandmother. It made her feel closer to her somehow by going there. She looked around the dusty old attic for hours. Something caught her attention in the corner. It was an antique trunk. She knew that she'd seen it before many times, but she never opened it. Now for some reason she wanted to know what was inside. Maybe it would make her feel closer to her grandmother. Jenna opened it up and found it full of books and papers. She looked around at all of the old papers. She picked up a book that had diary written on the front. Could it really be her grandmother's diary? She sat there on the floor holding the book, with a tear in her eye, when she was suddenly startled by the sound of the door bell.

Jenna walked back downstairs to see who it could possibly be. She opened the door to a handsome, rugged looking man. He had dark brown hair and he had to be at least six feet tall. He was tanned and muscular and gorgeous.

Jenna's heart felt like it stopped beating and she found herself taking a step towards the stranger without realizing it.

The stranger smiled and put his hand on top of Jenna's which was lying on his broad chest. Jenna snatched her hand away.

How had her hand gotten on his chest? She thought to herself.

With a chuckle he said, "I'm Jacob Masters. I knew your grandmother and I wanted to pay my respects to you."

Jenna thought she knew everyone that her grandmother knew. She had never seen this man before. Although she wished she had. She stood there thinking what a sexy man he was and wondering where those thoughts came from.

"I find it extremely hard to believe you were close to my grandmother. I've never heard her mention your name before."

Jacob stood at the door. He knew it would take a lot to get inside the house. Elena had told him how cautious Jenna was.

"I understand you're skeptical of my

44

friendship with your grandmother, but I assure you, I knew her well. Elena made me promise to come here and protect you when she died."

Jenna still had her hand clinched onto the edge of the door. "Okay, you say she wanted you to protect me. From what?"

"Not what. Who." He answered without emotion.

Jenna couldn't read him. She tried to get some kind of feeling about him, but she couldn't. She was torn between letting him in and making him leave. The old saying *keep your friends close and your enemies closer* kept popping in her head.

"Alright. I'll invite you in to talk. I want to know how you knew my grandmother and who you are suppose to protect me from."

Jacob followed Jenna into the house and into the kitchen. "Aw, you are making cinnamon apple tea."

Jenna spun around. "How could you possibly know that?"

"It was Elena's favorite. I had tea with her many times." he answered.

Jenna was beginning to get angry. "This is just crazy. I have lived with my grandmother almost my whole life. I spent every waking moment with her. We lived together and we worked together. Don't you think I would have noticed if you were coming and going around here? You're acting like I'm stupid or something."

"Jenna, that isn't my intention at all. If we had wanted you to see me then you would have. I have been here every day since the first day that you came here. I've been watching over you your whole life."

"What are you talking about?"

Jenna felt confused and scared. Not because she thought this man was lying but because she was terrified he was telling the truth.

Suddenly Jacob went invisible. "This is what I mean." Then he reappeared as quickly as he had disappeared.

Jenna drew in a sharp breath. "What the hell?"

Jacob knew what a shock this must be for her. "Let's sit down and I'll explain everything."

With a hand that wasn't quite steady, Jenna poured them both some tea and walked over to the table to sit down. She wanted to know everything.

"Okay, tell me what is going on."

Jacob sat down and stared at his cup of tea trying to find the words that would make her understand.

"Jenna, I've known your grandmother for many years. My father was her protector and my grandfather was her mother's protector as I am your protector. Your family and my family are tied to each other."

"What do you mean protector?" She was completely confused.

"I am here to protect you from evil."

"This is Snow Hollow. There aren't any evils in Snow Hollow." She was certain of that.

"Jenna, I know this is all hard to believe, but you need to take me serious. This house is more powerful than you know. Your grandmother was one of the most powerful witches there ever was."

"Okay, if she was so powerful then why did your father need to protect her?"

"My family is the most powerful warlocks around. We are even more powerful than your family, which is why we are your protectors. Let me explain. This house has been passed down from generation to generation in your family. Your family only has girls, hence you and your sisters. My family only has boys. We are destined to one another. If a member of my family only has one child then he is destined to the eldest girl from your family. If we have matched numbers then we are destined to the closest age. My family only had one son."

Jenna choked on a mouthful of tea and coughed uncontrollably.

"Excuse me, but are you saying that we are destined to be a couple? I think I should have a choice with who I spend the rest of my life with. There is a flaw in your theory though. For that to be the case, then my grandmother would have married your grandfather. She didn't. We would be related and not able to be destined to one another!"

Jenna felt proud of herself for finding the hole in his crazy, little theory. But it was short lived as he ignored her and went on.

"As I said, this house posses a tremendous amount of magic and power. Your family draws some of its power from this house. You don't know any of this, but your grandmother kept Snow Hollow safe from demons, vampires, evil warlocks anything that came to harm the innocent people of the town. As far as our grandparents go, they decided to stay friends only. He protected her until the day that he died and the rules changed. Instead of his destiny to love her it was now his destiny to protect her."

Jenna couldn't help but wonder why she never knew any of this.

"You were not supposed to know anything until you turned twenty six. That's when the girls in your family come into their powers fully. I'm sure you have been aware that you possess powers. You have always known things before they happen and you know that you can do spells. You have noticed little things over the years and have always been aware of the fact that you are different. I know that Elena taught you basic spells and simple things from the time you turned into a teenager.

As you know, I said I've watched over you. You have slowly been getting your powers year by year, but it's at the age of twenty- six that you actually get your full powers. That's why you weren't able to do much growing up and Elena always made it seem like fun and games. She was planning on telling you everything days before she died. We spent many hours discussing how we would tell you."

Jenna was creeped out by the fact that he had been watching her all these years. She felt her face flame as she thought that he might have seen her naked or doing things that were private.

Seeming to understand where her sudden embarrassment came from he quickly added, "Jenna, I would never take advantage of my gifts or treat you in such a manner. I watched over you with your Grandma's knowledge and permission always."

Jacob watched as a look of relief passed over her face. For now he would keep to himself the few times when he had been unable to stop himself from comforting her in her times of need.

Trying to change the subject, Jenna asked, "What kind of danger could I possibly be in?"

"I'm not sure. I can't get a good reading on it yet. All I can tell you is that the underworld is buzzing with talk. The news of your grandmother's death has traveled fast. I think I have it narrowed down to two possibilities of an attack. We have the demon angels. They are warlocks, but not as strong as my family, but stronger than you at this point. We'll start training you tomorrow. The other possibility is the Night Stalkers. They are a band of vampires. Your grandmother was very powerful as I've said, but this house also possesses power in itself. So if it can be taken over by evil it will strengthen their power. All they have to do is get you out of the way. Your sisters have never shown any interest in magic or this house. They may never come into their powers since they never try to use them. You're different. You are more powerful. You are a lot like your grandmother, which is why you can't deny this. You just need to let me teach you before it's too late."

Jenna's head was spinning in all directions. "Okay, for arguments sake lets say that I believe all of this. I need some time to think this all over. You have just thrown an awful lot at me all at once. I think I want to go to bed for the night. Seeing as you could pop in and out and I wouldn't know, I guess you might as well pick a room and stay until we get this all sorted out"

"I understand completely Jenna and I'm sorry I had to spring all of this on you. We will talk more tomorrow."

Jenna snuggled into her bed as she gazed at her grandmother's diary; a diary she never knew existed until moments before when she found it on her bedroom table.

Dear Jenna,

If you are reading this, then I'm no longer with you. Please always remember though, that I will always be with you. I know that you feel sad and alone right now, but that isn't the case at all. By now you must have met Jacob. You can trust him with all your heart. I'm sorry that I never got around to explain all of this to you, but Jacob will help you through your time of need. Trust him and let him teach you my ways. You must at all cost protect this house. It is your namesake. I know you don't understand everything right this minute but you will in time. Just know that I love you with all of my heart and I will always watch over you. You will find the answers that you need in

this house. Jacob will help you through this.
Trust him and you will come to love him.

Love always,
Grandma

Jenna dropped the book to the bed in disbelief. Her grandmother had just confirmed everything that Jacob had told her. Jenna looked up. "What am I supposed to do grandma? I can't do this alone. I need you."

It wasn't long before Jenna had dozed off. She tossed and turned repeatedly. Everything was dark and foggy. She couldn't get to the house. Every step she took forward sent her two steps back. Some force field was keeping her from moving. She cried out. "Help me. Help me." She couldn't see anyone around her at all. What was happening? Then out of the darkness she saw a shadow of a man. She couldn't make out who it was or what he looked like, but he was there.

The shadow figure moved his face close to hers and said. "Leave this house now or you will die."

Jenna screamed as she jumped out of bed. It was too real. It couldn't have been a dream. She walked around the room and then glanced out of the bedroom window. There across the street under the huge oak tree, she saw the same shadow figure starring up at her window.

"Jacob! Come quickly."

Jacob came running into the room. "What is it Jenna?"

"There. Look. He's there." She pointed

out the window.

Jacob walked to the window but saw nothing. The man disappeared as quickly as he had come. Even though Jacob didn't see the man, he knew he was there. He walked over to Jenna and rubbed her arms in a comforting gesture.

"Try to get some sleep and we will talk in the morning"

Jenna nodded. After Jacob left she was sure she wouldn't sleep this night. She just wasn't sure if it was because of the shadowman she'd seen or because of her memories of Jacob's large hands rubbing her.

Chapter 5

Jenna woke up the next morning feeling as if she didn't sleep a wink all night. Jacob's large hands had won the sleepless bet. She had lain there for hours with crazy thoughts running through her mind. His touch had almost felt familiar.

She walked over and started fixing some hot tea on the stove. She never was a coffee drinker. She was getting the eggs out of the refrigerator when she turned and saw Jacob standing there.

"You nearly scared me to death. You have to stop popping up like that."

With a boyish smile he said, "Sorry...

it's a habit."

Jenna finished fixing their plates and walked to the table.

"Okay, I need you to be honest with me. That wasn't a dream that I had. Was it?"

"No Jenna, it was very much real. He was trying to scare you out of here so he wouldn't have to battle you. He doesn't know exactly how strong you are yet. He was fishing for information last night. If you let him take over this house, he also takes over this town. Evil will take over and all of your friends will most likely die. I'm sorry to drop all of this on you, but you need to hear the reality of the situation. I no longer have the luxury of letting you mull all of this over. I need to start your training in order to make sure you're ready for what's coming."

He looked at her with eyes filled with determination. "Are you ready?"

Jenna thought about all he told her. And then she thought about her Grandma who had been her anchor for all her life.

"Okay, let's get started. I'm not going to let him scare me into giving up grandma's house. This isn't what I expected my life to be about, but if this is what is asked of me, I'm ready to fight."

Jacob looked across the table at her. "This isn't going to be easy. We need to get you trained in fighting so you can defend yourself against your attacker, but you also need to get you magic skills into shape too. You are a witch by nature. All we need to do is teach you how to use the skills that you already have."

Jenna wasn't sure how she got mixed up in all of this, but she knew she owed it to her grandma to give it her best. It was her legacy.

She spent the next few days working out with spells and spending hours training in kick boxing with Jacob. She couldn't help but think what a great trainer he was. She was surprised to find that she could move things without even touching them. She had never done that before. All she had to do was think of something and she could make it happen. Jenna was finding her new talents to be very interesting. She was also finding Jacob to be very interesting as well. She couldn't help watching him when he was working out beside her. She liked to watch his muscles flex and pull as he worked up a sweat.

Jacob pulled her out of her musings.

"Okay, now it's time for your next lesson. I want you to harness all of your energy into the palm of your hand. This will create an energy ball that you can then throw at your enemy. I want you to try and hit the target that I have put up for you."

Jenna thought and thought and nothing happened. She was starting to get frustrated. "This isn't working."

"Keep trying, Jenna. Think harder. You need all of your energy to form a ball in the center of your palm."

Jenna was getting madder by the minute. The madder she got the bigger the ball was getting. She was actually doing it. She looked at the target and sent her ball towards it. She hit the target with no problems.

"Oh my god! Did you see that? That is so cool. I can't believe that worked."

She ran over and threw her arms around Jacob in excitement. "I'm sorry. I guess I got a little excited."

Jacob's smile faded and fire burned in his eyes.

"It's okay we all get a little excited once in awhile." He reluctantly detached himself from her arms. "Why don't we take a little break? I'll fix you lunch."

Jenna laughed. "You are going to fix me lunch?"

"What is so funny about that? I'm an excellent cook." He defended himself with a smile.

As Jenna walked into the kitchen she turned to Jacob and said. "I'm going to go take a quick shower before dinner if that's alright with you. I'm all sweaty."

Jacob swallowed a bit hard. "Sure, go ahead. I'm going to start lunch."

Jenna walked to the bathroom and started her shower. She got in and let the hot steamy water run over her body. She washed her long black hair and the shampoo ran down her breast. The water was very relaxing and Jenna wished she could stay in there all night. Jenna felt like all of her senses had suddenly come alive. *It must be the training.* Jenna thought to herself. Her training involved discipline and concentration.

It seemed like an eternity when Jenna

heard. "Is everything okay in there?"

Jenna snapped out of her thoughts. "Oh, yeah, I'll be right out." She turned the water off and got out. After quickly dressing and running a brush through her hair she went to the kitchen to find Jacob.

He had made homemade beef stew and grilled cheese sandwiches. The table was set and he had poured them some ice tea.

"Everything smells great." Jenna said as she sat down and started to eat. "So tell me a little bit about yourself. I hardly know you and you live with me."

Jacob took a sip of his tea. "For starters, as I said, I'm a warlock. My family has been around for centuries as well as yours has. I am very powerful, but I can't fight these evils alone. I need you. They will team up and that will be too much for me to handle on my own, but with you together we can't be beat."

"Why did I not know that Snow Hollow is full of evil demons and things?" Jenna wanted to know. She didn't understand how she could have lived her whole life not knowing that her grandmother had been fighting demons her whole life.

"Don't feel bad. Not many people know. It's because your grandmother with the help of my family kept Snow Hollow safe. The townspeople never had to worry, but now that she is gone if we're not prepared, evil will take over."

Jenna felt a shiver run up her arm. She wasn't sure that she could do this. If she was ready to face the things he kept saying were coming. She missed her grandmother very much and she knew deep inside that she didn't have a choice.

Jenna finished her lunch without another word. She had too many thoughts running through her mind right then. She needed to be alone to sort through the changes that were taking place in her life.

She stood up, "Thanks for a wonderful lunch. I need to be alone for a little while to soak all this in. I'm just going to explore the house for a while. I'm finding all kinds of things that I never noticed before."

"I understand completely, Jenna. Let me just say, that I think you may want to start at the end of the main hallway behind the floor length painting of your grandfather."

Jenna stood there with an odd look on her face. "What are you talking about? What about the painting?"

"If you pull the frame towards you it will open a secret pathway."

Jenna was stunned. She has lived in that house for twenty years and didn't know about a secret passage. "I feel like such an idiot. Why didn't I know about a secret room?"

Jacob could see the hurt in her eyes. "Please don't feel bad. It wasn't time for you to know all of this. How could you just know? I'll tell you. You couldn't. Unless somebody showed you, nobody would know. Don't beat yourself up about this."

Jenna walked away kind of saddened. She wondered what else about her grandmother she didn't know. When she made it to the end of the hall she found herself standing there staring at the painting as if it were about to do tricks. She walked up to it and pulled it like Jacob instructed and sure enough it opened right up. She followed a long hallway down a darkened tunnel. It was a little scary for her, but she knew that Jacob wouldn't have sent her if it were dangerous. She realized that she trusted him.

She made it to the end and there she saw what looked like a den. It had book shelves from the floor to the ceiling. There was a desk and to one side was a table with what looked like chemistry flasks and things. Jenna was amazed at all the stuff in there.

She walked over to a huge book sitting on a book stand in the middle of the floor.

Jenna walked over to it and opened it up. She couldn't believe what she saw. It was a book of spells. Her grandmother actually mixed spell. How could she not know this about her grandmother?

It saddened Jenna to think she didn't know her grandmother as well as she thought she did. Tears started to fall from her face as she sank to the floor.

"Don't cry my dear." The voice of Elena said.

Jenna looked around the room, but saw nothing. "Grandma?" She said with a shaky voice. "Is that you?"

Slowly a beautiful light was forming in the middle of the room. Jenna could see her grandmother appearing in the center of the room.

"Grandma! How is this happening?"

"Jenna, honey. By now you should know that anything is possible. I know you are confused, but I've been watching you. I can see how well you are training with Jacob. He's a good man. You can trust him. I can't stay but just a minute. I just wanted to tell you that I love you and I'm always here with you. You are about to face some very big challenges, but together with Jacob you will handle them. Read these books in this room. They will teach you everything you need to know. I love you."

She vanished as quickly as she came.

Jenna sat there in the middle of the room crying. "Come back. Come Back. I can't do this alone." The tears where coming down like rain.

"Jenna. You aren't alone." Jacob said as he sat down and put his arms around her. "You will never be alone."

He sat down beside her and pulled her into his arms. Jenna looked up at him and then laid her head on his chest. The feel of him arms around her made everything seem okay for a few minutes.

Jacob held her tight. "I'm here with you and I will never leave you."

Jenna leaned up and kissed him gently on the lips. She didn't know where that came from, but for some reason it felt right. Jacob's arms tightened for a split second and with a small sigh he stood and held his hand out to help her up.

"We should get back to training now."

Deep down Jenna knew he was right

but part of her wished they could stay there a while longer.

Chapter 6

The days flew by with Jenna learning more and more every day. She felt like she could defend herself but she wasn't ready to try just yet. She needed to build up her confidence level a lot. She knew things were going to get bad soon, but she wasn't ready for it just yet.

She went into the kitchen to fix something to eat. As soon as she walked into the kitchen her stomach tightened up. There standing in the middle of the kitchen was a demon waiting to attack.

Jenna was scared to death, but she couldn't show her fear. She ran behind the counter dodging energy balls right and left. She jumped up and threw her energy ball right into the demons mid section. It was a perfect shot. The demon turned into dust before her very eyes. She had just destroyed her very first demon. The adrenaline was flowing through her veins. She felt a sense of empowerment about her. Jenna couldn't wait to tell Jacob what had happened. It almost felt too easy though.

She was walking up the stairs when she heard Jacob talking to somebody.

"Everything is going according to plan. Don't worry. I've taken care of everything."

Jenna didn't know what to think. She could feel the pit of her stomach hardening. What was he talking about? Who was he talking to? Should she trust him? What had he taken care of? Her head was spinning. She didn't know what to think. Had he been playing her for a fool this whole time, but why? She turned to run back down the stairs. Jenna tripped and fell. She kept falling and falling. Each step hitting her harder and harder until total blackness took over.

Jacob heard the noise and ran to her as quickly as he could. "Jenna! Jenna! I'm coming. Hold on."

He ran to her side. He checked her pulse and found that she was breathing. That was a good sign. He picked her up and carried her to the bedroom. Jacob laid her gently on the bed.

He went to the bathroom to get a damp wash cloth. He laid it softly on her forehead. "Jenna, come on honey. Come back to me. I can't do this without you. I need you."

Jenna couldn't move. Her head felt like it could explode at any minute. She wanted to ask Jacob what he had been talking about. What plan was working? Should she trust him? She couldn't move her mouth to say anything. She felt so tired. Maybe if she took a little rest she would be able to talk later.

Jacob paced the floor night after night. He had his father check her over. There was nothing they could do to get her to wake up sooner than her body wanted to. It was a waiting game at this point. Jacob sat on the bed beside her. He wanted to help her more than anything. He knew that he was in love with her, but he couldn't tell her until the battle was won. He couldn't distract her from the fight she was about to fight.

He sat by her bedside gazing down at her thinking she was the most beautiful person he had ever seen. He leaned over and moved her hair from her eyes and gently kissed her forehead. "Everything will be okay, Jenna. Trust in me and trust in us."

***

Jenna moaned as she tossed and turned. The room was dark and she didn't see Jacob anywhere. She tried to get up, but the movement made pain shoot through her head. She laid back down still unsure of what exactly happened. She knew that she had to get up though. She had to protect the house.

She wanted to see if her powers still

worked. "Energy ball." She yelled as she held out her hand.

Before her very eyes she saw the ball forming. "Go away." She said and it disappeared.

She rolled back over on her side to rest a while longer. She knew everything would be fine.

The next day Jacob came to her room to check on her and he found her bed empty. "Jenna! Where are you?!"

Jenna came walking out of the bathroom. "I'm fine. We have work to do."

"Jenna, you need to lie back down"

"I'm fine Jacob. Let's get started."

Jacob wasn't sure what had gotten into her. "Can you first tell me what happened? One minute, I'm on the phone with my father and the next minute I hear you falling down the stairs."

"Your father?" She said.

"Yes, I called him to tell him that everything was going according to plan. I let him know that the training was coming along nicely."

Jenna felt as if the wind had been knocked out of her. She had acted so foolishly and almost cost her, her life. How could she not trust Jacob? Her grandmother told her that he could be trusted. She should have listened. Jenna always could be on the stubborn side.

Jenna wanted to change the subject quickly. "I lost my footing on the top step. The next thing I knew I was tumbling head first down the whole flight of stairs. I'm okay now though. I'm sore, but we have to get to work. We are running out of time. That's what I was so excited for when I was running up the stairs. I had just defeated a demon in the kitchen."

"What!" Jacob walked closer to her. "What happened? Tell me exactly what happened."

"Well, I was going to the kitchen to start some lunch and he was there in the kitchen. He was going to use an energy ball on me, but I reflected it back to him and killed him. I thought it was odd that it was as easy as it was."

Jacob rubbed his chin for a minute. "They are sending out their less experienced demons to test you. They wanted to see how much you knew. This means they are preparing themselves. The batter will be soon. Tell me everything you remember about the demon, so I can figure out which group he belonged to."

Jenna spent the next few minutes telling Jacob everything that she remembered about the demon, which wasn't much. The whole battle took about a minute. She threw an energy ball at him and he vanished. It was almost too easy.

The rest of the day was spent training and conjuring spells for Jenna to use during battle. They were all very simple and fast to say spells. The faster the better when you are in the middle of fighting a demon or vampire.

Chapter 7

Jenna went to bed that night not before looking out the window and seeing the shadow of the man again. Why was he out there every night? Why didn't he just make his move? It didn't make sense to Jenna. She laid down not being able to sleep for hours.

When she finally fell asleep, the dreams started taking over. She almost hated to fall asleep anymore. She could see the shadow man coming towards her. The fog would creep in and she would find herself running as fast as she could, but she wouldn't get anywhere. The man kept getting closer. She tried to scream but nothing came out.

She tossed and turned, fighting with her blanket until she finally screamed as loud as she could. She sat up in her bed and the tears started falling. *Why is this happening to me?* She screamed to the air.

Jacob came running in. He saw her sitting up in her bed crying. He ran to her and put his arms around her.

"Jenna. I'm here. You're safe."

Jenna looked up wiping a tear from her face. "I'll never be truly safe again. My whole world has been turned upside down." She laid her head on her knees and continued crying.

It broke Jacob's heart to see her like that. He touch her hair softly with his hand

and stroked it gently. He pulled her into his arms and held her tightly as they sat on the bed together.

Jenna looked up into his eyes. His touch felt familiar. She leaned up and kissed him on the lips.

Jacob returned the kiss with more passion than she had given. He had loved her for a long time now, ever since she had blossomed into a woman. He kissed her again each time lasting longer than the one before.

Jenna felt safer than she had in a long time. She knew that she loved Jacob. She fell fast asleep in Jacob's arms and slept through the rest of the night with no nightmares. It was the best night's sleep she had had in a long time.

The next morning Jenna woke up alone

in bed. Had she been dreaming? Did last night really happen? She got out of bed and quickly got dressed. When she started down the stairs she smelled bacon cooking.

Jenna walked into the kitchen and saw Jacob standing at the stove cooking.

Jacob looked up and smiled. "Hey there. I didn't want to wake you. I hope you're hungry." He walked over and took her into his arms. He kissed her until she was slightly breathless.

Jenna felt all her worries float away. Last night was real. "Yes, I'm starving. I can't wait."

Jacob laughed. "Okay, it will be ready in a few minutes. When we are done eating we have to get back to training. You need to practice on writing spells."

"Why do I need to know that?" she wondered.

"Well Jenna. You don't know this, but your family has the unique power of writing spells. Any spell that you say will work. You can turn objects into other objects. People into frogs. Anything that you say in spell form will work. It's a very powerful tool. I will teach you how. Once you get the hang of it, it will be easy for you."

They walked into the secret room of Jenna's grandmother's to look through all of her old books. Jacob thought that it would be the best place to start.

"Okay, Jenna. You should start here. Read through these books and practice spells. That's really the best way to learn. You kind of have to just jump in and do it. I'll leave you alone for a while. If you need anything call for me. I won't be far."

Jenna was a little overwhelmed at first, but she knew she had to practice. The more she knew the better it would be. She picked up the book and practiced for hours with everything from making books to fly to moves objects from one place to another.

She had mastered spell making and the art of fighting. She knew deep down that she was ready for the battle of her life time. However, she also knew it wasn't something she was exactly happy about doing. She could die.

Chapter 8

Jacob came to Jenna one night after dinner. He found her standing by her bedroom window looking out. He knew something was wrong. She had been acting strange all day. "Jenna, is everything okay?"

"Not really. I think it's time for the battle. The shadow man has been out there all day and he's still there. I'm not going to sit here and wait for him to kill me. I'm going out there and starting the battle myself."

Jacob ran over to the window to look out. "Jenna, you can't do that. That's what he wants. If you leave this yard, you won't be as strong as if you fought him here. You need him to come to you. You need to force him to come to you."

Jenna knew the best thing for her would be to calm down and plan her strategy. It was the only way she would win the fight.

There was a loud crash coming from downstairs. It sounded like the house was being torn apart.

"Jacob, I think it's started." She ran down the stairs.

Jenna saw a red faced demon with horns coming from his head throwing furniture everywhere. "Energy ball." She threw it right at him, but he dodged it.

The demon returned one that hit Jenna right in the stomach. She was thrown across the room crashing into the wall.

"Jenna!" Jacob yelled as he ran to her.

"I'm okay." She stood up and fired another energy ball that hit dead on that time. The demon disappeared in front of them.

"Why did I kill him with one ball, but all he did was knock me down?"

"You are a lot stronger than he was. Somebody is just testing the waters."

Jenna knew that the night wasn't going to end easily. She had to come up with a plan and fast. She had studied the spell book for weeks and made a number of vanishing potions. All she had to do was get close enough to the shadow man and she was confident that she would vanquish him.

She walked over to the front door and opened it wide as Jacob stood there starring at her.

"What are you doing?"

Jenna looked at him hoping that he would understand. "Don't tell me what to do Jacob. You aren't my boss."

"What are you talking about?"

Jenna glanced over her shoulder then back to Jacob. "I said go home. I don't want you here anymore."

Jacob had no idea what was going on.

Jenna glanced over at the door and saw the shadow man slowly creeping in the door. Her plan was working. She knew if she made the shadow man think that she was distracted he would make his move. She needed him to come in a little closer and then she would have him.

"Jenna, what the hell are you talking

about?"

Jenna glanced over his shoulder and saw that the Shadowman was holding his hand out ready to strike. She pushed Jacob out of the way.

The Shadowman spoke in a voice that was filled with evil. A voice that knew what pain and suffering was.

"You have no idea what you're dealing with. I'm more powerful than you can imagine. This house will be mine and I will fill it with putrid darkness until the essence of that bitch Elena and her vile apple tea is eradicated from this earth."

Jenna couldn't contain the rage the his words evoked and she threw an energy ball at him without much thought.

The shadow man dodged it with ease

and returned one that Jenna dodged in return.

She needed him to get just a few feet closer to her so she could throw her vanishing potion on him. She took a few steps closer to him and held up her Grandma's diary that she had grabbed while upstairs.

"I have a deal for you. I'll give you Elena's diary with all her secret spells and in return you let Jacob and I leave unharmed to start a life of our own."

"Jenna! What are you doing? You can't give him that diary" Jacob yelled.

The Shadowman threw an energy ball at Jacob knocking him back to the ground. "Mind your own business." The he turned back to Jenna. "What makes you think I'm stupid enough to fall for your tricks?"

"No tricks. You can kill me and Jacob. I know that. I'm only beginning to learn my powers and I can't fight you. I don't care about Snow Hollow so it works out perfect for both of us. Plus I will promise to never come back to Snow Hollow and if I do the deals off, you can kill me."

"I require more than that." He looked at Jacob. "Kill your lover."

Jenna took a moment to contemplate the offer and then shrugged. "All right. I only put up with him because I thought he was kind of cute."

Jenna stretched her hand holding the diary out towards the Shadowman.

Jacob struggled to his feet and looked at Jenna, his eyes filled with hurt and betrayal.

Jenna slowly slipped her hand in her pocket to get the vial. The Shadowman had his greedy eyes glued to the diary.

From his angle, Jacob saw what Jenna was doing and he understood her game. Even though he was frightened for her, he couldn't help but admire her courage.

The Shadowman took a step closer and Jenna threw the vial right in the center of him.

For a millisecond a look of astonishment passed over his face and then the Shadowman simply disappeared.

Jenna let out a sigh of relief as she watched the demon disappear.

Jacob walked to stand at Jenna's side. She looked at him with a big smile on her face.

"I did it Jacob. I saved Grandma's house and I vanquished the Shadowman."

Jacob smiled. "Yeah, you saved the day Jenna. I'm really proud of you. But that wasn't the most awesome thing you did just now."

She looked at him with her eyebrows raised in question. "What could be more awesome than beating a freaking demon, a creature from the underworld?!"

With a straight face he said "You said I was cute."

"Oh...you jerk..." She laughed and pushed him, but he caught her hands in his and brought them to his lips.

"I love you Jenna...I've always loved you"

Jenna felt that love deep down in her soul.

"I love you Jacob...and I always will."

Book Two

Jamie's Story

Chapter One

The road back to Snow Hollow was long and tiresome. Jamie Addison hadn't been back since her grandmother died. She loved her sister Jenna, but she never wanted to embrace her life as a witch.

She always thought if she stayed away from Snow Hollow then she could run from her gift. It didn't work.

She moved away, but the demons still found her. They seemed to have a way of knowing when a witch is around, and she spent the past few years fighting demons anyway.

Now she must return to ask for her

sister's help. Jamie had a secret she'd kept from her sister for close to two years and now she had no choice but to tell her. How was she supposed to tell her sister she had fallen in love with the one thing that was forbidden, a demon?

Jamie decided to make the trip on her own to convince her sister that Danny was different. He chose to lead a good life. He would never hurt them. Jamie wanted more than anything to marry Danny, but she couldn't unless she got Jenna's blessing.

Jenna, being the eldest of the Addison witches, had to give her permission or the Witches' Counsel would condemn the marriage and banish both Jamie and Danny to the darkest part of the underworld.

Jamie always wanted to lead a normal

life, but it simply wasn't in the cards for her. She spent most of her adult life living in a small quiet town in the middle of nowhere. She didn't want to fight demons on a daily basis, and ironically she fell in love with one.

The long driveway to the Addison house was fast approaching. Jamie's stomach tightened. It was going to be hard to explain to Jenna and her husband Jacob how she could possibly love a demon. She knew they wouldn't understand.

She brought the car to a stop and got out.

Jamie saw her sister running down the porch steps to meet her. "Jenna I'm so glad to see you!" she said as she put her arms around her sister and pulled in her in tighter. She truly did mean it. She had missed her sister.

"I'm glad you're here. I've missed you." Jenna took her bag and started towards the house. "Jacob will be glad to see you too. I hope you can stay awhile. You didn't really say on the phone."

The nerves were creeping back. She rubbed her hands on her jeans as she thought of how to answer. "I'm not sure really. I took a couple days off work and thought I would come for a visit. "

"Lets get inside before Jacob comes looking for us."

The girls laughed as they ran up the steps.

Jamie knew she had her work cut out for her in trying to convince Jenna and Jacob that Danny was a good guy despite the fact he was a demon.

Jamie walked in the house and the memories started flooding back. The days turned into years since she was last there, but the place hadn't changed at all. She felt her grandmother all around her.

She walked around the front room looking at everything in sight. The smell and feel of the house was completely the same as before.

Jamie turned to face the door, pointed her finger and said, "Close." The door didn't close.

Jamie looked at the door again and repeated, "Close." Again nothing happened.

What was going on? Why weren't her powers working? Maybe she was just tired. It was strange, but she didn't worry.

Jamie was nowhere near as strong as Jenna, but she could hold her own in battle. She was blessed with the gift of spell writing. She could create a spell in a split second. She spoke and it happened.

When she walked into her room to put her things away she dropped to the bed. Her eyes began to get teary. She looked around the room she grew up in and as she picked up a picture of her parents, she signed as she thought she couldn't even remember them. She was only four when they died and she came to Snow Hollow to live with her grandmother.

She had a good childhood though. Her grandmother raised her right. Nevertheless, she still missed having her parents in her life. It was her grandmother who taught her all about magic.

Elena, was a witch. She spent her life protecting Snow Hollow and she taught her granddaughters to do the same.

Jamie took out her cell phone to call Danny. She wanted to let him know she made it alright.

After three rings she heard, "Hello."

"Hi,Honey. I just wanted to let you know that I made it here with no problems."

"I'm glad you called. I was worried." Danny said. "How is it going? Have you asked her yet?"

Jamie bit her lower lip. "Not yet. I just walked in the house. I'm really tired though. I may not get into it until tomorrow. I don't want to fight about it tonight."

"Okay Babe, I love you and I don't

mean to rush you, but I think you should really talk to her tonight. If you wait she might try to talk you out of it. I don't want anything to come between us. I want us to be together forever."

"I love you too and you are right. I shouldn't wait. I'll talk to her tonight. I'll call you tomorrow." Jamie held the phone for a minute before hanging up. She had only been gone a few hours but she missed Danny already.

She knew she needed to get downstairs for dinner soon. She wanted to help Jenna in the kitchen.

As Jamie left the room she checked her powers again. She looked at her cell phone she on the dresser. She reached her hand out and said, "Phone." The phone didn't come to her. She did it again and nothing happened. Jamie walked over and grabbed the phone with her hands somewhat shaking.

When she got down stairs she saw Jenna cooking dinner at the stove. The memories came flooding back of her grandmother cooking.

The house smelled the same as it always did growing up. Jenna made the same apple cinnamon tea that Grandmother Elena made.

Jamie looked over at Jenna. "Something smells good."

Jenna looked up with a smile. "I'm glad you're here. I don't want to make you mad, but I need to talk to you about something."

Jamie knew that Jenna knew the

reason she was here. Her sister had always known things long before anyone else. It was a sixth sense . "Okay what do you want to talk about?"

"Jamie I can feel something attached to you. What is going on? Do you feel different in any way?"

Jamie paced the room not wanting to answer.

"What is it Jamie?"

"Well. My powers aren't working. I've tried a couple of times since I got here and nothing happens. What do you think it is?"

Jenna wasn't sure exactly. "When was the last time you were able to use your powers?"

Jamie thought about it for a minute. "I don't really know. Since I've been with

Danny, you know the guy I told you about, I haven't really had to fight any demons."

"Tell me more about Danny."

"Wait a minute," Jamie yelled. "You don't think he has anything to do with this? He loves me and I love him. That's why I'm here."

"What are you talking about, Jamie?"

"Jenna come sit down so we can talk." Jamie grabbed a cup of tea and headed for the table." Jenna followed.

As they sat down a worried Jenna said. "Tell me what's going on."

Jamie started her story. "Well before you get upset, I need you to listen to the whole story. I met Danny one night when I was fighting a demon. I got knocked down and the demon was going to kill me. Right before he threw an energy ball, Danny jumped in front of me and threw his own energy ball at the demon and defeated him."

"That's great Jamie, but what are you not telling me?"

"Okay, but don't freak out. Danny is a demon."

Jenna jumped up from the table. "Jacob! Get down here now!" she yelled for her husband who was their family protector.

"Jenna, calm down. Danny has changed his ways. He is good not evil. He loves me and he wants to marry me. That's why I'm here. I need your blessing."

"There is no way in hell I'm giving my blessing for my sister to marry a blood sucking demon. It's not going to happen."

"Jenna you aren't being fair. You don't

even know him."

Jacob walked in as the voices escalated. "What is going on in here? You two are sisters. You shouldn't be fighting like this."

Jenna turned to Jacob. "Jamie is in trouble. She is in love with a demon and her powers are gone. She can't get them to work at all."

"Everyone calm down. Jamie come over here to me." Jacob motioned for her to come to him.

"Danny couldn't have had anything to do with this. He loves me." Tears were forming in her eyes as she tried to defend the love of her live.

Jacob could see the bind on her powers. She had a red glow all around her. It couldn't be seen by anyone other than a protector. He knew this wasn't good.

"Jamie I think you need to sit down. We need to talk."

"Okay." She agreed.

"Listen to me carefully Jamie. Somebody bound your powers and you have a love potion put on you as well. Somebody is trying to get to you Addison girls and the Addison house. I'm sorry but the love you feel for Danny isn't real. You are in serious danger. He could have killed you and since he didn't we know he wants something more from you. I'm sorry."

Jamie didn't know what to believe. There was only one way to find out.

"Jacob, **Truth be Told**" She put a truth spell on him. It would only last a few minutes. He wouldn't know.

She spent the next few minutes asking him questions about the love spell and the bind on her powers.

It was all true.

Chapter Two

Jamie lay on her bed in tears. How could this be happening to her? Everything she thought was real was a spell. Her whole world was turned upside down. She didn't want to believe it, but she had not other choice.

Jenna walked up to her door and lightly knocked. "Jamie. Can I come in?"

"I guess."

Jenna walked over to her sister and laid her hand on her head. "Oh Honey, I'm sorry. I know you are devastated. Jacob called his cousin Drake to come protect you. He will be glued to you until we defeat

Danny. Your powers will come back when he is defeated. Until then you won't have any powers at all. I don't want you left powerless and unprotected. Drake will be here in the morning."

"How could I have been so stupid?" Jamie started crying all over again.

"You weren't stupid. You have been under a spell. Jacob is working on a reversal for the love spell, but you won't get your powers back until we defeat the demon that did this to you. We will have to set a trap for him and make him believe that you still believe he loves you. We don't want him to know that the spell has been broken. Drake will be with you every step of the way. You will never be alone."

Jamie sat up and put her arms around

her sister. She felt safer already.

She laid back down on her bed and thought about Drake. She hadn't seen him since she was a teenager. She remembered him being quite attractive.

Drake lived away and only came to visit during the summers, but he always came over to play when he was in town.

Jenna went back downstairs to find Jacob. She found him in the living room hanging up the phone.

"Did you get a hold of Drake?"

"Yes. He will be here first thing in the morning and he won't leave her side for a minute. She will be okay. We'll protect her." He pulled Jenna into his arms and held her.

* * *

Jamie woke up the next morning feeling little worried about how things would go.

She went into the bathroom to take a fast shower. She couldn't believe that she fell for Danny's tricks. She was confident that Jenna, Jacob, and Drake would be able to defeat Danny, but she still felt stupid. She leaned her head against the shower wall.

Jamie got dressed and went downstairs to wait for Drake. It wasn't long before she heard the door bell ring. As she opened the door t–she gasped. Standing in front of her was the most handsome man she had ever seen.

He was six feet tall with long black hair, and his muscles bulged under his white t-shirt. *That couldn't be Drake.* She thought.

" Drake?" Jamie asked as she opened the door the rest of the way.

Drake walked in. "Yeah and you must be Jamie." He smiled. "Where is Jacob?"

"He is in the study trying to figure out a spell to kill Danny." The smile faded from her face as she thought about how he'd taken advantage of her. How could she have fallen for it?

Drake could see it bothered her to talk about Danny. "Don't let it bother you. You are under a spell. You couldn't have known what he would do."

Jamie fought back the tears. "I should have known. I'm an Addison. There is no excuse for me letting a demon get that close to me. He could have attacked Snow Hollow and taken the house."

"Your sister and Jacob will always protect this house. You don't have to worry about it."

"But you don't understand how hard it is for me not to run to him. The spell is weakened since I'm hours away, but I can still feel it tearing at me. I know what he did was wrong, but my mind still wants to love him. I'm being pulled in all different directions. I need to get out of her. I think I'm going to go for a walk to clear my head." Jamie started to the door.

Drake moved quickly to stop her. "You can't go by yourself. That's why I'm here. Remember? I'm here to protect you. I'll go with you."

Jamie wiped a tear away from her eye

knowing that she couldn't argue with Drake and not really wanting to anyway. They walked out the door together.

As she walked down the path to the pond, Jamie looked around at all the butterflies fluttering in the air. She held her hand out and thought as hard as she could for one to land on her hand, but nothing happened.

"When I was little the butterflies used to flock right to me.

"It's okay Jamie. You will get your powers back. I promise."

There was something about Drake that made her feel safe. It was strange.

"Come with me. I'll show you where I used to play in the garden when I was a child. My grandmother used to stand at the back door and watch us girls running in the yard. I can remember all the butterflies landing on my arms while I played."

Thinking back brought a smile to her face.

Drake stood there staring at her thinking how beautiful she looked. He vowed to protect her with everything he had. He wouldn't let the demon get her.

"Jamie maybe we should go back to the house. I don't want Jenna and Jacob to worry too much."

Jamie knew he was right. She didn't want Jenna to worry.

When they walked in they saw Jenna standing in the kitchen making potions.

"What are you making?" Jamie asked.

Jenna looked up from the pan she was

stirring. "I'm trying to make a reversal to the love potion, but I don't think its working. I've been doing spells all day, but the spell put on you is very strong. I can't seem to break it."

"I have faith in you. You'll get it. Maybe I can help. Although my stomach feels like it's doing cartwheels. I feel love for him but hate for him too." Jamie knew deep down that if anyone could break the spell it was Jenna.

Jamie went upstairs to take a long hot bath. It had been a long day. She added bubbles as the water filled up. She slowly took her clothes off and let her hair down. As she sank down in the hot steamy water she could feel her worries float away. It may only be for a few minutes but at least she had those minutes.

She lay there in the bath tub thinking

about the day. Thoughts of Drake filled her head. He was very sexy, but how could she be thinking about Drake if she was under the love spell. Maybe the spell was getting weaker since she wasn't around Danny. Could that be it?

Jamie stayed in the water until it got cold. When she finally got out she was too tired to do anything but go to bed.

As she lay in bed, dreams of Drake took over. They were walking in a field of wild flowers holding hands and smiling.

All of a sudden dark clouds started to settle in. Everything was black and Drake disappeared. Jamie looked all around but found nothing but darkness. What was going on? She yelled but nothing came out. In the mist of the blackness she could see Danny appearing. As he walked closer she tossed and turned in her bed. Her beautiful dream was quickly turning into a horrible nightmare. She sat up in the bed immediately and looked around. Everything was the same as before she went to sleep. It had all been a bad dream.

She laid back down and tried to sleep. That wasn't going to happen.

Chapter Three

Jamie got up and went downstairs to the kitchen. She knew just what she needed. A hot cup of apple cinnamon tea would ease her worries. She could already smell the scent as she walked down the stairs. She knew Jenna would have some made.

She poured herself a cup and grabbed the morning paper as she walked to the table. She glanced down at the paper, nothing new in Snow Hollow. Jamie thought she would go out to the barn and train for a while. She may not have her powers but she could still fight and it would give her something to do.

As she was kicking the bag she saw Drake walk in. "Good morning." She smiled at him.

"What did that bag do to you?" He said with a chuckle.

"Well I'm pretending it's Danny."

"Ah, how's that working for you?"

Jamie laughed. "Pretty well actually. What's on your agenda for the day?"

Drake raised an eyebrow.

"Oh, come on. You don't have any plans for the day. Do you just plan to sit across from me all day starring at me? I think we will both go crazy. We have to find something to do until Jacob breaks the spell on me and we go after Danny."

Drake thought for a minute. "Okay, I guess we could go somewhere. Jacob and

Jenna probably won't like it, but I see your point. You can't just sit here. So how about we go to dinner and a movie?"

Jamie burst out laughing. "Did you just ask me on a date?"

Drake couldn't help but laugh. "I guess I did. Do you have something better?"

"As a matter of fact I do." She smiled. "I've wanted to go down to the lake for awhile. How about a paddle boat ride? Then we can get something to eat afterwards."

Drake smiled. "That sounds like fun. Lets go."

They spent the next few hours on the lake talking and laughing.

Jamie was happier than she had been in a long time. How could she let a demon bind her powers and put a spell on her? Her smile faded.

Drake looked over at her. "What's wrong?"

"Nothing. I just don't know how I could have let this happen."

"You are too hard on yourself. If you hadn't let it happen, we never would have met. I have been enjoying myself the past couple of days."

She smiled at him. "I have been enjoying myself too."

They got out of the lake and docked the boat. When they were walking back to their car a demon, who had been watching and waiting all day, jumped out of the shadows.

The demon shot a fire ball at them. It missed them and hit the fence behind them.

The fence made a loud crash as it broke into many pieced.

Drake shoved Jamie out of the way and threw a fire ball back. He missed. It landed in a bush catching it to fire instantly.

The demon threw one of his own back.

Drake dodged it and this time he didn't miss with his return fire.

The Demon turned to ash before their eyes.

 He turned and ran to Jamie.

"I'm fine," she said. "But if you hadn't been there I would have been a sitting duck."

"You will get your powers back. I promise and I won't leave your side until you do."

Jamie looked into his eyes and saw

nothing but love. She felt safe with Drake around.

Jenna heard Jamie and Drake come home and she knew something was wrong. She ran outside to meet them. "What happened?" Jenna asked.

" I'm okay. Drake kept me safe. We were attacked by a demon. He wasn't strong and Drake defeated him with ease. I think he was sent here to see how protected I am."

Jenna looked over at Jacob. "What do you think?"

Jacob nodded. "I agree. I think Danny is sending some of his clan to check on things. He must know we figured out what he did."

Jamie looked a little worried. "Okay so what do we do to prepare?"

Jacob walked closer to Jamie. "First tell

me everything you know about Danny."

"Well I don't know how much I can help. I'm sure that everything he told me was a lie."

"I agree," Jacob said. "What I want to know is what you learned about him on your own. How does he fight? Is he left handed or right handed? Things like that. He apparently knows a lot about you girls. Now we need to learn as much about him as we can."

Jamie fought back tears. "If he knows so much about us, then he must have chosen me for a reason. He must have seen that I was the weakest link."

Drake walked over to her. "Don't think like that. It doesn't matter what he thinks. I don't think you are the weakest link at all. I think you're great." He reached over and gently took her head in his hand. He leaned down and softly kissed her on the lips.

Jamie kissed him back. She felt like she was floating. She forgot for a minute that Jenna and Jacob were standing there watching.

"Sorry to interrupt." Jacob said. "But the love spell is broken. All it took was true love's kiss and apparently the two of you have really become close over the past few days."

"Do I have my powers back?" Jamie was excited.

"No, I'm sorry. We have to break the bind on them. The only way to do that is to kill Danny." Jacob explained.

Drake put his arm around her. "We will get your powers back. Don't worry."

It didn't make Jamie feel better knowing the people she loved were going to go out looking for a demon to kill. Most of the time they came looking for them and they were prepared for a battle. Things would be different with Danny. He would be ready for them. She couldn't let them do it alone. She had to find a way to help.

***

Jamie went to bed that night racking her brain with ideas. She needed to go to Danny. She needed to fight him off before her family went after him. He wants them to leave the house unprotected to go after him. She wouldn't let that happen.

Jamie got up in the middle of the night, threw her clothes on, and left the house quietly. She planned to sneak attack Danny and throw potions on him. She could kill him without actually having her powers. It was simply a matter of tricking him into thinking she didn't know his plan. She planned to seduce him and while she had his mind on other things she would hit him with a potion. She had to try and protect her family. She couldn't let him hurt the people she loved.

She quietly got in her car and drove out of the driveway. She would be with Danny in a few hours. She had everything planned out in her head. It had to work.

Chapter Four

Jamie walked in the door of her and Danny's apartment. She glanced around looking for him. As she walked down the hall she heard him talking on the phone.

"Danny! I'm home and I have good news," she said as she walked in the bedroom.

Danny hung the phone up and smiled at her. "Babe. I missed you." The whole time he was thinking of ways to kill her. He could see the minute she walked in that the love spell was gone. Somebody had outsmarted him, but he thought he could still turn it back around on her.

"Jenna gave her blessing. We can get

married and she can't wait to meet you." She threw her arms around him. She was giving her act one hundred percent.

"That's great Babe. Why don't we go there now. I can't wait to meet her." *I can't wait to kill her and take the Addison house,* he thought to himself.

Jamie wasn't sure if her act was working or if he was doing one of his own. She couldn't get a good read on him. She could tell that she felt no love for him at all. The love spell was completely gone. All she felt for him was hate.

"Sure let me just call her and let her know that we will be there in a few hours to celebrate. I can't wait."

Jamie knew that Jenna would be mad when she found out what she had done, but this way she could bring Danny to them and they could be prepared.

She picked up the phone to call, but it was Drake that answered instead of Jenna.

Jamie cheerfully said, "Hi, Jenna."

Drake was a little confused. "What the hell are you talking about and where are you?"

"Yes, Jenna he was so excited to hear the news. I told him as soon as I walked in that you gave us your blessing."

Drake was scared now. "Jamie! Get out of there. Get away from him. I know you think you are helping, but this is dangerous."

"Danny can't wait to meet you and Jacob. So we are getting in the car right now to come there to celebrate. I told him that we could fire up the grill and have a great time.

He can't wait."

Drake understood what she was doing and he prayed that the plan worked. "Jamie. I love you. You have to be careful."

"I love you too. See you in a few hours."

Danny stood there watching with his head spinning. He couldn't believe he was going to get into the Addison house that easy. His plan had worked. He knew there was probably a trap waiting for him so he had to play it smart.

"Let's get going, Babe. I can't wait to plan our wedding."

Jamie knew she had him now. She would save the potions until they were back in Snow Hollow. She would have back up there. Nothing could go wrong.

The car ride was quiet other than the sound of the radio. She had too much going through her mind to talk and she assumed that Danny did as well. She knew he was planning his attack.

As they pulled in the drive, Jamie saw Drake come running out.

As she was getting out, she turned to Danny. "Danny this is my cousin Drake." She shot Drake the look that meant he better follow along. She had to get Danny in the house.

Danny nodded. "It's nice to meet you. " He said with a fake smile. He thought that he had them good.

"She's inside," Drake said as he motioned him to follow.

They slowly walked inside careful not

to let Danny out of their site.

"Danny, come on. I want to show you everything."

Danny didn't argue. He was finally inside the Addison house. He wanted to see every corner of it. Then he would plan his move to kill them one by one starting with Jamie. "Great. I can't wait to see where you grew up. I want to see everything." He faked another smile.

Drake hated the site of seeing Jamie standing that close to a dangerous demon.

Jenna came in the room ready to fight. She stood in front of him and said. "Energy ball!" and threw it right at him

Danny dodged it and grabbed Jamie in the process. He was much more powerful than that. It would take more than one energy ball to kill him. He grabbed Jamie by the throat and jerked her off the ground.

Drake ran toward him. "Let her go!"

Danny threw a fire ball and hit him in the stomach.

Drake fell to the ground immediately.

"Drake! No!" She yelled as she wiggled free and ran to him.

Danny ran behind a chair. and started throwing fire balls at them. He was missing right and left and the fire balls were hitting the walls and the chairs. Fire was breaking out in the living room in patches.

Jacob ran for a fire extinguisher as Jenna continued to fight. He started putting the fires out.

Jenna returned fire, but with Danny behind the wall it was hard to find him.

Danny poked around the wall again.

Jenna threw an energy ball that hit him in the arm.

Jamie watched him fall back a little. She grabbed a potion bottle and threw it on it.

Jacob jumped in and threw another energy ball.

Danny fell to the ground and disappeared.

Jamie could feel her powers returning. She turned to the table and yelled. "Vase." The vase started floating towards her. She grabbed it and set it back down. "I have my powers back. Thank you everyone. I love you all. I couldn't have done this without you."

Drake slowly got up, walked over to

her and put his arms around her. The pain
shot up threw his stomach. He needed Jacob
to heal him.

Jacob walked over and ran his hand
across Drake's burn and it started to
disappear.

Drake looked up at Jacob. "Thanks
man, that burned like you wouldn't believe.

"No problem. That's what I'm here
for." Jacob smiled.

Jamie, who was in his arms the whole
time, snuggled in closer. The feel of his
embrace made her feel even safer. She didn't
want to leave him ever.

Drake loved the feel of her in his arms,
but he couldn't help but think it was all going
to end. Now the danger was gone. Would she
still love him?

Drake looked up at her. "Can we take a walk?"

Jamie nodded.

When they walked outside and down the path, she turned to Drake. "What is it? I can tell something is wrong. I'm sorry I didn't tell you my plan."

"Well that did scare the hell out of me, but I understand and I'm not mad. I know we haven't known each other that long, but I know that I love you and I need to know where I stand with you. Are you still leaving in a day or two?"

Jamie felt like the wind was just kicked out of her. She hadn't thought about it until now. She had a job and a life waiting for her back home, but the thought of leaving Drake saddened her. She didn't know what to do.

"I don't know." She said without thinking.

"Well I must not mean that much to you if you don't know. I know I love you, but I understand if you need time to think. You have been through a lot. I'm going to go for now. You should rest. Call me later." Drake kissed her then he turned and walked away.

"Drake I love you!"

He didn't turn around. He just kept walking. He didn't want to pressure her.

Jamie sat down on a rock and started to cry. How could she let him just walk away? She loved him, but she did have a lot to think about. She had a great job and friends. She sat there gazing off into the horizon when she saw something.

Appearing before her eyes was a white

glowing figure. She hadn't seen it before. It kept getting closer by the minute until it was right in front of her.

"Grams. Is that you." Jamie couldn't believe that she was seeing her grandmother Elena right before her eyes.

"Hi Sweetie. I only have a few minutes. I just wanted you to know that I have always been here with you. I have been watching over you. You did excellent today. It was very brave of you to do what you did. I know you are hurting right now with all these decisions you have to make, but your heart will tell you what to do. You know what you want out of life. I love you my dear."

"I love you too Grams," Jamie said as she watched her grandmother disappear as quickly as she had appeared.

Jamie knew what she wanted. She wanted Drake. She had to find him. She had to tell him that she loved him.

She ran up the path to find him only to find Drake, Jenna, and Jacob all standing up against the wall in the living room. They weren't moving at all. She had to see what was going on.

She looked in the window and saw a demon with red blood shot eyes and muscular arms standing there freezing them in place. "Oh here we go again" or something like that." She had to do something.

Jamie decided that a surprise attack was the best option. She could distract him so he would let go of his freeze on the others. She had to do something fast.

Jamie flung the door open as hard as

she could.

The demon turned quickly still keeping the other three frozen.

Jamie shot the demon with an energy ball, but he was too powerful. He didn't die. Jamie landed a roundhouse karate kick to his stomach.

The demon dropped to the ground and released his hold on the other three.

Drake threw an energy ball that knocked the demon through the coffee table shattering it into several pieces.

Jenna and Jacob both fired at the demon at the same time and watched the demon disappear.

"Thanks Jamie. If it hadn't been for you, I don't know what would have happened." Jenna hugged her sister.

"How did he get inside and freeze all three of you at the same time?" She didn't even think that was possible.

"We had our backs turned. We were talking about the lunar eclipse. We have a lot of planning to do for it. We didn't even hear him come in."

Jamie hadn't even thought about the huge upcoming battle with the most powerful demons of the underworld. of the underworld. It happened once a year.

The underworld trained for it all year. It was the main goal of the underworld to get the Addison house under their control. They all longed for the powers the house held.

The lunar eclipse was the perfect night. It was when all their powers aligned perfectly. It was a difficult battle to fight, but they always won and Jamie knew they would win this year as well. She was confident.

"I forgot about that," Jamie said.

The three of them looked at her.

"What? I've been under a spell remember? I'm out of it now though and I'm ready to train harder."

Drake raised an eyebrow at her. "Does this mean you are staying for awhile?"

She walked over to him and kissed him gently on the lips. "How does forever sound?"

"That sounds perfect to me," Drake said as he lifted her up and kissed her more intensely.

"Well I need to go train for awhile. I have been under that spell for so long I think it weakened my powers some."

Drake agreed. "Yes, I think you should

train. I'll help you if you want. We can start with physical training in the barn on the punching bags, and then I think you should do magic as well. We need to strengthen your powers as well as your muscles."

***

They headed to the barn.

Jamie trained hard for the next few hours. She was exhausted and really wanted to do nothing more than sleep.

Drake observed how tired she was. He could see her movement slowly. He felt bad that she pushed herself so hard.

"Jamie I think you are doing too much too soon. Why don't you call it a night. I'll come back over tomorrow and we can train some more."

Jamie was tired. "Okay. I'll see you

tomorrow."

She walked up to the house and upstairs. She wanted nothing more than a quick shower and then her soft bed.

She sank down into her bed and fell fast asleep.

Chapter Five

Jamie woke up the next morning feeling very refreshed. A horrible weight was lifted off her shoulders. They had defeated Danny and she was in love. Her life was finally turning around.

She knew she had more training to do but she couldn't wait to see Drake. She smiled just thinking about him.

She didn't want to seem too pushy or desperate so she decided not to call him. Instead she went outside to practice with her magic and spells. She needed to strengthen her powers after breaking the bind on them.

She spent hours doing spell after spell.

When she had decided to call it a day she heard Drake walk in.

Jamie smiled instantly. She felt like a school girl in love. "Hi."

"Hey, how's the training going. I didn't want to bother you earlier since you were training. I want you to be ready for the big battle. I don't want anything to happen to you."

Jamie walked over to him and kissed him softly on the lips.

Drake pulled her in closer and returned the kiss. His kiss moved from her lips to her neck . His kiss moved back up to her lips. Then he said, "I thought I lost you when you went after Danny yourself. I was scared to death."

"You will never loose me," Jamie said

as she pulled him closer. Her lips touched his and they stayed like that for seconds.

Drake looked down at her and moved her hair out of her eyes. He kissed her on the forehead. "I love you."

"I love you too, Drake."

Jamie knew she had a big battle coming, but for now, she wanted to enjoy the moment.

"Jamie, come back to my house and I will cook you dinner."

Jamie laughed. "You cook?"

Drake smiled. "I'm a good cook thank you very much. I want to spend a little alone time with you. Just the two of us."

"I'd love to come over. Let me tell Jenna that we are leaving so she doesn't worry."

They left and went over to Drake's house which was only a few miles down the road. The driveway was long and paved with white dogwood trees lining both sides.

When they got to the end of the driveway a beautiful white cottage revealed itself. with a wrap around porch. The porch had a small wooden two-seater swing on it hanging.

Jamie   fell in love the minute she saw it. She jumped out of the car and ran up to the red rose bushes by the porch. She held her hand out to touch one of them. She thought they were beautiful.

Drake held her hand gently and led her into the house.

"This is my house. It's small, but I like it.

"I love this place," Jamie said.

"Okay you go sit down and relax, and I'm going to cook you a great dinner."

Jamie smiled as she went to sit on the porch swing. "Okay, I'll be out here."

Drake went into the kitchen and started dinner. He went out the back door and started the gas grill. He threw a couple of steaks on it and then went back into the kitchen. Drake got out a bottle of wine and but it in an ice bucket to chill. He started making a salad and grabbed a loaf of French bread off the counter and started cutting it up.

As he finished setting the table the steaks finished cooking. He took them off the grill and brought them in.

Jamie came walking in. "Something

smells good," she said.

"Sit down and enjoy." Drake handed her a glass of wine.

"Wow this is delicious," Jamie said.

The two of them sat there for over an hour talking and getting to know each other better.

"Why don't we move to the couch where it's more comfortable?"

They went into the living room with their wine and snuggled down on the couch.

Jamie felt safer and more at home than she had in a really long time.

She knew she was right where she wanted to be. She couldn't imagine ever being without Drake.

The End

Book Three

Jackie's Story

Chapter One

"Energy ball!" Jackie Addison yelled as she held out her hand to catch it.

She caught the ball and threw it as fast as she could at the demon waiting to throw one back at her. She hit him square in the chest and he disappeared before her eyes. She had defeated yet another demon.

It was somewhat of a lonely life she lived, but it was the life she was destined for. It was her job to fight demons and keep people safe without letting anyone know she was a witch. It was hard to keep the secret though. She knew one day she would find true love and it would be worth all the time she spent fighting.

Jackie only had a few days left before she had to meet her sisters back at Snow Hollow. The eclipse would be there soon and the three sisters had to be together for it. It was a very powerful night for the underworld. They thrived on the night of the full moon. It would be the perfect time for them to attack both the town and the Addison house. It would take the three of them together to fight them off. Of course Jenna's husband, Jacob, would be there and Jamie's husband ,Drake, would be there. She often wondered when she would find her mister right. Would it be somebody magical or a common human. You never knew when love would find you.

Jackie went home to her quiet

apartment which she shared with her black cat. After she threw a fast dinner in the microwave she ran upstairs to take a quick shower and change. She always felt creepy and dirty after fighting demons. She jumped in and washed up fast and then went back downstairs to eat her probably now cold dinner.

Jackie was kind of restless that night. She decided to go to the all night gym to workout. Maybe she could beat out her frustrations on one of the punching bags.

She pulled her car into the dark alley and grabbed her gym bag to walk in. She heard footsteps coming up behind her but when she turned around there was nobody there. She turned to walk again and again she heard the foot steps, but as she turned around they stopped. She was starting to get angry.

"Okay come out and show yourself. You have messed with the wrong person tonight."

Out of the shadows came four big guys walking toward her. They all looked like the kind of guys you wouldn't want to run into in a dark alley if you weren't a witch, but for Jackie she looked at them and almost felt sorry for them.

The leader of this gang of roughnecks walked up to her. "Isn't it a little late for a cute little thing like you to be out. You could get hurt."

Jackie looked him dead in the eye. "I think that if the four of you don't get out of here and leave me alone you will leave here crying after pissing your pants."

The men didn't really know how to respond, but one of them in the back pushed his way through. "Well we have a feisty one here. I want her first."

The men started to walk closer to her.

Jackie had really had enough by now. It was after midnight nobody was around to see her so she was going to let these men have it. She drew back her hand to throw an energy ball at them.

"No, Don't!" A voice from the shadows came.

Jackie spun around to see who was there.

Walking toward her was the sexiest man she ever seen. He was tall with long blond hair. His muscles outlined his shirt perfectly.

Jackie liked what she saw, but she still had some things to deal with. She turned back to the men. "I'm going to give you one more chance to leave before I make you leave."

One of the men chuckled a little.

The mystery man now standing behind her said. "You better listen to her and run. I called the cops and they will be here within minutes."

That's all it took before the men took off running. They didn't want to get involved with the police.

Jackie turned to the stranger. "I could have handled those men just fine. I didn't need your help"

The stranger started to laugh. "Oh, I

know you could have Ms. Addison. I've been watching you for a while now. I see you fight every night, but those are demons you are fighting. Those men even though they were asking for it didn't deserve to die. They may have deserved to go to jail, but the energy ball you were about to zap them with would have done more than jail."

Jackie was a little curious now about who this man was. "Okay, you seem to know so much about me. Who are you?"

"My name is Ricky and I have been watching you night after night defeat one demon after another. You are very powerful."

"Why have you been watching me and why are you up at those hours of the night?"

"Maybe we should go for a walk. It's a long story."

Jackie eyed him up and down for a minute. "Okay, let's go for a walk around the park."

As she walked, she looked up at this man walking next to her wondering what his story was. "Ricky is it? I think it's about time for you to explain yourself."

"Yes, it's Ricky. Short for Richard. I am mesmerized by you. I watch you every night fight off those demons with ease. You hardly break a sweat."

"Okay Ricky, you still aren't telling me why you are watching me and why you are up at those late hours. I only fight demons when everyone else other than demons would be in bed. So are you telling me that you are a demon?"

"No I'm not a demon, but I don't know

if what I am is better or worse in your opinion. I'm a vampire."

Jackie stood there shocked for a minute. Why didn't her senses tell her that he was a vampire? "What? You are a vampire?"

"Yes. That's why I'm up all hours of the night. Now let me explain before you kill me. I'm not like the others. I don't kill people. I think I proved that earlier when I stopped you from killing those humans. I need blood to live. That is true. So I have to feed. I only feed on animals."

Jackie had never met a vampire who didn't kill people. She was thrown aback a little. There was something about him that told her he was telling the truth. She could see it in his eyes. "Tell me a little more about yourself."

"Well my name is Richard Ellington. I am 110 years old. Now that times are modern, I shortened it to Ricky. When I was twenty-three I was driving home from work one night and had a flat tire. I started walking to the nearest gas station and when I did I was attacked. I don't know why they chose to turn me instead of simply killing me. I have never known the answer to that question. So I have lived a long lonely life keeping this deep dark secret. Then I saw you and I knew that I could tell you everything since you had your own secret. I needed somebody to talk to."

"So nobody knows about you?" Jackie was trying to wrap her mind around everything she had heard.

"Nope. Nobody. So your turn. Tell me

about you. How is it that you fight demons every night."

"Let's see. Where do I begin? My name is Jackie Addison and I'm a witch."

"Wait a minute. You are an Addison Witch?"

"Yes. I'm the youngest of the Addison girls."

"I have heard about you three. I don't go to the underworld world anymore, but when I first got turned I didn't know what else to do. I heard all about your family. You three of course weren't born but it was destined that you would be. I heard your name one night. I knew it was Addison but I didn't know it was The Addison. I had no idea you were an Addison witch. Wow."

"Well that's me. My sister Jenna lives

at Snow Hollow in the Addison house because she is the oldest. Her and her husband Jacob protect the town. Together they can't be beat. They don't really need help except on the lunar eclipse of course. There will be too many demons for the two of them to handle on their own. So I picked a city that I new would be full of demons for me to fight. Granted New York City has way too many for me to actually protect the city, but the way I see it is; if I can kill a few a night it's a few less that the city has to worry about."

Ricky couldn't believe he was actually talking to an Addison witch. He heard many stories about their powers over the years. "I am very glad I met you. I would like to see you again if that's alright with you."

Jackie was excited about the idea of seeing Ricky again. It was a little strange that she spent the past few hours talking to a vampire when she has spent most of her adult life killing demons and vampires but there was something different about Ricky. "I would love to see you again. It's almost sun up now though, so I better let you go home. Here's my number. Call me."

Ricky took the phone number with a smile. "I will. Talk to you soon." He turned and walked away.

Chapter Two

Jackie walked into her apartment with a smile on her face. Thoughts of Ricky filled her head. How could she even be thinking about a vampire in that way? It went against everything she had been taught over the years. Vampires were bad, but he was different. She wanted to get to know him better.

She was tired after staying up all night talking. The thought of sinking down in her bed sounded wonderful right then. She changed into some comfortable pajamas and went to bed.

Her dreams were filled of Ricky. She

just met him. How could she have such strong fillings for somebody she just met?

Jackie woke up refreshed after hours of sleep. It was the middle of the afternoon now. She had to go into work for a few hours, but not long. She was a real estate agent and she had a house to show to a couple downtown. It wouldn't take long. She was confident that they were going to buy and the commission on the deal was going to be a really big one. It was a nice, big, fancy two story brick house with seven bedrooms. The selling price was one million dollars. Her commission would be ten percent of the price. It was enough money to hold her over for a while. She needed this sale since she was going to take time off soon to prepare for the lunar eclipse battle back in Snow Hollow.

Jackie left to meet the couple to show the house. She spent the next few hours pointing out all the great qualities of the house and pitching her deal hard. She was good at her job. She could sell just about anything. It came easy for her. In the end she got the deal she was looking for. The house sold and she went back to the office to drop off the paper work.

Her boss pretty much let her pick and choose her hours. She was the top selling agent in his company so he catered to her needs.

She dropped the paper work off and told her boss not to forget that she would be taking off a few weeks for vacation. She told them that she had a family reunion to go to and then different family things to do. With her sales record her boss didn't even question the time off.

Jackie left the office suddenly hungry. She realized that it was now evening and she hadn't had anything to eat besides a quick bagel on her way out the door on her way to work. She was starving. Jackie drove over to her favorite dinner.

The waitress came over to take her order. "What can I get you?"

Jackie glanced at the menu out of habit, but she already knew what she wanted. "Give me a sweet tea, a bacon cheddar burger with everything and a side salad with Ranch dressing. Thanks."

"Wow! That's a lot of food for such a small woman."

Jackie spun around to see who was

standing behind her. She turned to see the handsome face of Ricky starring back at her. "Well if it isn't my night walker. Aren't you out a little early? It's not quite night yet."

"Ah yes, but the sun has set. You should know by now that it doesn't have to be pitch black outside. I just need the sun to be not as bright."

Jackie pointed to the empty seat in front of her. "Have a seat. Do you want anything?"

"No I'm good." Ricky said with a smile.

"Well I'm not one of those women who acts like I don't eat. I'm going to enjoy the huge burger that I just ordered." She laughed.

Ricky couldn't help but laugh. "Well I like a woman who knows how to eat."

Jackie's food came and she ate while

talking to Ricky.

* * *

Jackie and Ricky spent the next few weeks inseparable. She was slowly falling in love with him. It wouldn't be easy to get her sister Jenna to accept him. Especially after her sister Jamie had fallen in love with a demon after being put under his spell. He had almost killed Jamie and tried to take the Addison House. Jenna wasn't going to trust that Ricky was different. She had to have the blessing from Jenna before their relationship could go any further. The only way the Witches council would let an Addison Witch be with anyone other than a warlock was the relationship had to be approved by the eldest Addison girl which was Jenna.

Jackie was worried that Jenna

wouldn't approve since she didn't know Ricky the way she did. He wasn't like other vampires. He wouldn't hurt anyone. He fought demons side by side with her every night for weeks now. He wouldn't hurt her. She had to find a way to prove it to Jenna.

Ricky knocked on the door to Jackie's apartment. When she answered he asked. "Hey gorgeous do you want to go somewhere?"

Jackie thought for a minute. "I'm not really in the mood to go out tonight. How about we rent some movies and just come back to here ?"

"Sounds good to me, but is anything wrong?."

Jackie shook her head. "No nothing is wrong. I just want a nice quiet night in. No demons to fight."

Ricky understood completely. He could use a night off too. "Okay we have a plan." He smiled. "Let's go grab some movies."

The night had set in when they got their movies all picked out. As they walked out of the video store Jackie could feel the demon around.

She looked around in all directions but she couldn't see it. She knew it was there though.

She had parked her car around back in the empty parking lot. With nobody around to see, she would have no problem defeating the demon there with nobody to see, but she had to find it first.

Ricky looked around. "I sense it too, but where is it?"

Just then an energy ball hit Jackie in the arm. Her arm felt like it was on fire. She could see the burn on her arm and the pain was agonizing. She looked around and in a tree across the lot she saw it.

Ricky saw it too. He ran to the tree. With his super speed he was there in seconds. He grabbed the demon and bit him in the neck and it vanished. He had killed it. He turned back and ran to Jackie.

"Come on Jackie, we have to get you home before anyone sees you."

She got up and handed Ricky her keys. "Okay you drive."

"Do you want to go to the hospital?"

"No!" Jackie yelled. "How am I supposed to explain that I was hit with an energy ball from a demon?"

"Right. I wasn't thinking. Sorry."

Jackie felt bad for yelling at him. "It's okay. We just need to get home. I have a potion that will clear this right up. I'll be fine within minutes."

Ricky drove her home as quickly as he could. His heart was pumping. He didn't know if it was from fighting with the demon or seeing Jackie hurt. He had feelings for her that he couldn't explain. He met her only days ago, but he felt such a strong connection to her. He felt like he had to protect her even though he knew how powerful she was.

Jackie laid in the passenger seat in horrible pain. She couldn't take much more. As the pain took over she drifted unconscious.

Ricky pulled into her apartment

building and ran around to the passenger side of the car. He picked her up and carried her inside of her apartment. When he got inside he laid her on her bed, but he didn't know what to do. He didn't know how to make potions and he was sure that there wouldn't be a bottle labeled to tell him. He had to figure something out.

After getting her laid in bed he ran to the kitchen to look around. He had to get a healing cream on her soon or she would die. He glanced around and on the refrigerator he say a list of names and numbers. He had to call somebody. Who? He read the list and saw the name Jenna. That's it. Jenna is her sister. I'll call her. She will know what to do. She has to.

Ricky dialed the number and waited

for an answer. He heard somebody say hello. "Hello. Is this Jenna Addison."

"Yes. Who is calling please?"

"You don't know me, but I'm a friend of your sister Jackie..."

"What's wrong? Is she okay?" Jenna was scared.

"She was attacked by a demon tonight. I defeated the demon but Jackie was hit by a fire ball. She is unconscious but she said that all she needed was a potion. I don't know what potion she's talking about. I need help."

"Slow down. This is very important. Did Jackie say it was a fire ball or did she say it was an energy ball. There is a difference."

Ricky thought for a minute. "When it first happened, she called it an energy ball but on our way to her apartment she called it a fire ball."

"What does the burn look like?" Jenna asked.

Ricky ran to the bedroom with the cordless phone. "Okay, I'm looking at it now. It has a small burn with a really big black circle burn around it. What does that mean?"

"Okay it was an energy ball. This is much worse. What did you say your name was?"

"It's Ricky. Ricky Ellington. What do I do?"

"First you have to calm down. You did the right thing by calling me. I'll be right there."

Within seconds Ricky saw Jenna appear before him.

"What the hell?" Ricky jumped back.

"Hello, I'm Jackie's sister Jenna and you must be Ricky."

Ricky was a little shocked but nothing really surprised him too much. He was a vampire and he was in love with a witch. Things were far from normal in his life.

Jenna ran to her sister to examine the wound. She confirmed that it was in fact and energy ball wound. She ran to the kitchen and prepared the potion. She went back to the bedroom and rubbed it all over the burn.

Then she turned to Ricky. "She will sleep for a few hours but she will be fine. Let's go in the other room and talk."

Ricky took a blanket from the end of the bed and tucked Jackie in. He leaned down and kissed her forehead and turned to follow Jenna into the other room.

189

Jenna made a cup of tea and then turned to Ricky. "Okay what are you not telling me? The average Joe would be completely freaked out by all of this. So explain. I know you aren't a warlock or you could have cured her yourself. You aren't a demon or I would sense it. I am sensing something about you, but I'm not getting a good reading on you."

"Let me explain everything before you try to kill me."

Jenna looked at him strangely but she nodded her head in agreement.

Ricky blurted it out quickly. "I'm a vampire. Now before you say anything. I love your sister. I don't kill people. I only feed on animals and I fight demons with Jackie every night. I know you can kill me in a split second. I've heard the stories of the Addison witches. I know your power. I know that you are the most powerful of the three. I have no reason to try anything. I lead a lonely life until I met your sister. She treated me differently than most. I love her. I haven't even told her yet. When she got hit back there I was scared to death that I would loose her. That's why I called you. If I was any threat to her at all, I could have killed her in her sleep or not called you and let the energy ball kill her. I love her. Okay that's all I have to say. You can do what you have to do now."

Jenna stood there amazed at how a vampire was professing his love for her sister. She could tell he was different and that he wouldn't hurt Jackie. What she didn't know was how it could work, but that wasn't for her to say. Her sister was entitled to decide who she loved.

"Okay I believe you. I give you my blessing. Take care of my sister. I will see you both for the eclipse. We could use your help. I have to get back now. Check on Jackie every hour until she wakes up. She will be fine don't worry. If she had put the potion on the burn immediately it wouldn't have been as bad. I just wanted you to know that it isn't usually this bad. She should have taken some with her. If Jacob was here he could have healed it in a minute, but he's away on family business. Just know that she will be fine. She will sleep for a few hours but then the burn will be completely vanished and she will be fine."

Ricky was relieved to hear she would

be okay. "Thanks for coming to help me. I'll have Jackie teach me all these potions so I will be able to protect her myself next time."

Jenna said goodbye and disappeared before his eyes.

Ricky went to Jackie's side and lay his hand on her head as he sat down beside her.

Chapter Three

Ricky knew Jackie would be fine but he couldn't help but worry about her. He would feel better in a few hours when she woke up. He pulled a chair up next to the bed and sat down to wait.

Jackie tossed and turned. Her thoughts were filled of battles. She was fighting one demon after another in her dreams.

Jackie opened her eyes, jumped up. "I gotta go. I'm late."

"Jackie! Stop. You can't go anywhere right now. You're hurt."

Jackie looked over at Ricky sitting beside her. "What happened?"

"You were hit by an energy ball. You were fighting a demon and he hit you."

"Jackie looked at her arm. "Oh, yeah, I remember now. I was so stupid."

"No you weren't. These things happen."

Jackie wouldn't let herself off the hook that easily. "Yes they do happen but I should have had my potions with me and then it would have healed instantly. How did you heal me. Vampires don't have healing powers?"

Ricky stood up and paced a little as he rubbed his hands on his jeans. "Okay. Don't be mad, but I got your sister's number off your refrigerator. Jenna orbed here instantly. Which by the way scared the hell out of me. I was talking to her on the phone one minute and she was standing beside me the next."

Jackie started laughing. "Was she mad?"

"No. I explained that I am a vampire and hoped she wouldn't kill me. She was really cool about it."

"Well that's because you aren't a demon. My sister Jamie was under the spell of demon. She thought she loved him, but Jenna, Jacob,and Jacob's cousin Drake helped her break the spell. In the end Jamie and Drake ended up falling in love and got married. You will meet the whole family when we get there in a few days."

Jackie stood up and started smoothing out her shirt.

"What are you doing? Don't you need to rest or something?"

Jackie laughed. "No I'm fine now. The potion heals almost instantly. I'll have a small burn for a day or two but I'm all better. If I hadn't been so stupid and actually took it with me I wouldn't have been down as long as I was. Let go get something to eat. I'm hungry."

Ricky laughed. "Well I will watch you eat anyway."

Jackie went in the kitchen and made a sandwich. She was suddenly really hungry.

She looked up from her sandwich. "Okay when I'm done eating I have to get packed. We have to get to Snow Hollow. We have to train and make potions for the lunar eclipse."

"Tell me the truth, Jackie. How dangerous is this for you? Should I be worried?"

Jackie sighed deeply. "I won't lie to you, Ricky. We could all die. We have this fight every year. Every year we win, but there are no guarantees. Basically the demons attack in a pack and they are more powerful than usual, but even with that we are still much more powerful. So it isn't really that big of a deal. It's just that there are so many that it makes it a little harder. I do want you to know something though."

"What?"

"I love you."

Ricky smiled and pulled her in close to him. "I love you too."

Jackie kissed him and then pulled away. "Okay we have to get going. Jenna will be expecting us."

Jackie started packing her things for the trip. She would be in Snow Hollow for a few weeks so she had to be sure to get everything she would need.

Ricky left to get his things. He wouldn't be long.

Jackie packed the trunk of the car until it wouldn't hold anymore. She left room in the backseat for Ricky's things.

When he got back he loaded the car with his things.

They started the long trip back to Snow Hollow.

Chapter Four

After days of driving, the long tiresome trip was finally over. Jackie could see the Addison house coming into view.

She turned to Ricky. "There it is. That's the famed Addison house."

Ricky was in awe. "I've heard so much about this place. It's beautiful."

The car came to a stop and Jackie jumped out. She ran in the house.

"Jenna! We're here."

Jenna came walking into the living room. "Jackie. I'm glad you made it okay. Where is Ricky?"

"He's coming. Thanks for accepting him."

"Of course. He saved your life. I'm happy to invite him into the family."

Ricky came carrying in the bags. "It's nice to see you again, Jenna."

Jenna walked over and gave him a quick hug around the bags he was carrying.

Ricky looked up at her with a shocked look on his face. He could feel it. He knew Jenna was keeping a secret.

Jackie walked over. "Come on Ricky. I'll show you where my room is."

Ricky followed Jackie up the stairs giving a quick glance back at Jenna.

Jenna looked up at him. She knew he knew. She couldn't let him tell. Nobody could know until after the eclipse. She had to focus on the fight.

Jackie put everything away and then they went downstairs to work on potions with Jacob.

Jackie saw Jacob working at the stove. "Hi Jacob. I want you to meet my boyfriend, Ricky. He has come to help us fight."

"Jenna has told me all about you. It's nice to meet you."

Ricky held out his hand to Jacob. "It's nice to meet you too. Now explain to me all about this fight we are going to have. I'm new to all of this. I guess Jenna told you. I'm a vampire."

Jacob nodded. "Yes, she did. Well it's kind of simple to explain actually. One day of the year we have a lunar eclipse. The moon will be completely full on the night of the lunar eclipse. It is the one night that the demons draw extra power from the moon. It's the one night that they unite to attack the Addison house and the Addison witches. They figure they will take out their common enemy then they will battle each other for the house. So basically we have to work extra hard to defeat them."

Ricky ran his hands through his hair. "Okay. Let me get this straight. They are much more powerful and they will all attack at once. How can you win?"

Jacob understood how confusing it all was. "That's a good question. They are more powerful and they have numbers on their side, but any given day of the year, I and the Addison witches are more powerful. They still can't defeat us. Their plan is that they will hopefully kill one of us and then the next year it will be easier. So basically they don't plan to win an entire battle on one night. If they kill one of us then they have won for that year."

"I see. So what is the plan."

Jackie walked over to him. "The plan is to simply be ready. We have all the potions ready. We make them in bulk. So instead of throwing one bottle we will throw gallons at one time. We even have these guns that we built to shoot the potion out at them. It will be a crazy night but we will win."

"Well I'm going to leave you two to making potions and I'm going to take a walk around and explore." Ricky said.

"Okay, Babe. Have fun." Jackie gave him a quick kiss.

Ricky walked out back and saw the path leading to the pond. He followed it to the end and he saw Jenna standing at the pond with her hand on her stomach.

"How far along are you?"

Jenna spun around. "What?"

"I'm a vampire remember? I have senses. I know you are pregnant. How far are you?"

"You can't tell anyone. I haven't told Jacob yet. If he knew he wouldn't want me to fight."

Ricky understood. He wouldn't want Jackie fighting if she were pregnant. "Maybe you shouldn't. I know you are the strongest, but you need to protect your child."

"I need to protect my family and this house too. I can do both."

Ricky raised his voice. "What if you get hit in the stomach, Jenna. You can't do this and I can't keep your secret."

"If you don't want me to orb you to the underworld you better keep your mouth shut." She stormed off up the path.

Ricky kicked the dirt in front of him. *What am I supposed to do now? I can't keep this from Jackie. She has to know that Jenna shouldn't fight.*

He threw a couple pebbles in the pond while he tried to wrap his brain around the situation.

Jackie walked up behind Ricky. She knew something was wrong. "What's wrong?"

"Nothing." Ricky said as he quickly looked away. He couldn't look her in the eyes and lie."

"Ricky I know something is wrong. What is it?"

"I can't tell you. I know a secret but it's not my secret to tell."

Jackie was worried now. She could see it was tearing him up inside. "Ricky, Talk to me. Tell me what's wrong."

He paced back and forth running his hand through his hair. "Okay. I love you and I don't want any secrets between us. It's Jenna. She's pregnant."

"What? How do you know?"

"I sensed it when I first met her. She said if I told anyone she would banish me to the underworld, but I don't think she should fight. She hasn't told Jacob. She says she won't until after the eclipse."

Jackie turned and started running to the house. She wouldn't let Jenna put herself or her unborn child in danger.

She ran into the kitchen where Jenna and Jacob were finishing up the potions.

"Jenna, You aren't fighting."

Jenna turned around and saw Ricky walking in. "What are you talking about. What did he tell you?"

"Jenna, you shouldn't have asked him to keep your secret and you shouldn't have asked him to lie to me. That wasn't fair to him."

Jacob was looking back and forth watching the argument with no clue what was going on. "What are you two talking about."

Jackie looked at Jenna. "You better tell

him now or I will. It's too dangerous for you to fight tomorrow."

"Dangerous? Why?" Jacob wanted to know.

"I will be fine, but something wonderful has happened to us. I wanted to wait until after the eclipse to tell you. We are going to have a baby."

Jacob ran over to Jenna. He picked her up and spun her around. "This is wonderful. I'm going to be a father." Then it hit him what they were fighting about. "Oh my God. Jenna. You can't fight. You can't put our child in danger or yourself."

"Jacob, Honey. I will be fine. I can shoot a few demons without it hurting me."

"No. There are plenty of us. There's me, Ricky, Jackie, Jamie, and Drake. I can even call a few more family members to help out. I don't want you in this battle. Your number one priority is to protect our child."

Jenna could see how worried he was. "Okay. You win. I'll stay in the attic with a protection bubble around me. Nothing will get to me. I'll be fine."

Chapter Five
The Lunar Eclipse

The battle was here. The Addison witches had to defend the house once again. Only they would be one Addison short. Jamie and Jackie with the help of Jacob, Drake, and Ricky would have to protect not only the house but also Jenna.

They had to be sure no demon got anywhere near her. She was carrying a future warlock. A child created from the blood of a warlock and an Addison would be the most powerful being around. Demons would do anything to get their hands on that child.

They could turn it evil given the chance.

The stakes were much higher.

Jackie and Jamie started filling their bags full of potions.

Ricky and Jacob loaded all the guns.

Midnight was soon approaching and the battle would begin.

Fog settled in and the waiting game began.

Midnight struck and through the windows they saw the demons starting to trickle in.

They all went out in the yard for the battle.

Jacob put a protection spell on the house. No demon could get in without breaking the spell and it wasn't an easy one to break.

As the demons came closer the energy balls flew. Fire filled the sky around them. Fences were being shattered. Dirt was flying.

Drake and Jacob threw energy balls at the demons while Ricky shot potions at them.

Jamie yelled. "Energy ball." Then she threw it at the demon approaching her.

Jackie dodged balls right and left getting hit in the left once. "Jacob. I've been hit."

Jacob ran to her side. He ran his hand over her leg and the burn disappeared instantly.

The battle went on for hours before sun was starting to come up and the remaining demons had given up. It was a long tiresome battle but the Addison witches prevailed as usual. There was never any doubt.

They went inside to rest as they had saved the house yet another year and now they had more to celebrate. There would soon be a new Addison.

The Addison legacy will continue on with a new generation.

www.solsticepublishing.com

Contact information:

solsticepublishing@live.com

www.ingramcontent.com/pod-product-compliance
Lightning Source LLC
Chambersburg PA
CBHW060924180626
46817CB00004B/1378